By the same author

Vengeance at Tyburn Ridge
Yellow Town
The Bone Picker
Last Stage From Hell's Mouth
Dead Man's Eyes

Dead Man Walk

The authorities warned Jim Jackson that if he eve
Texas again then he wouldn't get out alive. But J
Searching for information about old friends incarcera
cruel Texas penal system, with intentions to bust the.
wherever they are.

When Jim foils a train robbery, he's suddenly a hero
hunted man. The death toll rises as Jim attempts to outrun
the authorities and the friends of the train robbers he ki
Meanwhile, there's still a prison break to engineer.

And there's also the matter of the beautiful and enigmat
Rosalie Robertson. . . .

Dead Man Walking

Derek Rutherford

A Black Horse Western

ROBERT HALE

© Derek Rutherford 2018
First published in Great Britain 2018

ISBN 978-0-7198-2596-5

The Crowood Press
The Stable Block
Crowood Lane
Ramsbury
Marlborough
Wiltshire SN8 2HR

www.bhwesterns.com

Robert Hale is an imprint
of The Crowood Press

CHAPTER ONE

She was a pretty woman, made prettier by the late afternoon light shining low across the plains and through the carriage window. The light lent her skin a golden glow that reminded him of the beautiful paintings he'd seen back east a lifetime ago. She wore a bonnet and fancy clothes, but her lips were tight, as if behind them she was gritting her teeth. Her eyes darted around the carriage. It looked as if she was waiting for something, and whatever it was, she didn't expect it to be good.

Jim Jackson eased into the seat opposite her. He'd spent an hour in the cattle wagon with his horse, making sure she was settled, reassuring her. He'd wondered about bringing her on the train but she hadn't been bothered at all. There were other horses in the wagon too, plenty of hay, and they all looked happy enough swaying very gently with the motion of the train, relaxing, letting something else cover the miles for a change. Most of that time he'd spent with the horse, Jim realized, had been for his own benefit, reassuring him rather than her. So eventually he'd left her to the company of the other animals and had worked his way back through the short train, looking for a quiet space where he could stretch out and get some sleep.

The train wasn't full, so he chose the quietest carriage. The woman was sitting in the corner on her own. He sat opposite

5

her. She looked at him briefly, smiled, and then stared out at the passing plains of Texas, the fields of cotton and cattle, the dark prairie, the smoke, sometimes white, sometimes black, blowing back from the locomotive.

He watched her for a while and once or twice, when she scanned the carriage, she caught him looking and smiled again. He felt he was making her nervous so he stretched out best he could, pulled his hat down over his eyes and tried to sleep, enjoying the sound and feel of the wheels on the tracks, the light rhythms that made him think of music he hadn't heard for a lifetime, not since he left his home all those years ago. He breathed in the smell of the smoke and occasionally the woman's perfume.

He was drifting into sleep when she made a quiet frightened sound. It was so slight that it almost wasn't there, but when he opened his eyes she had her hand over her mouth and was looking out of the window at a couple of cowboys on horses watching the train roll by. The train was slowing as it climbed a slight grade, but then it started picking up steam again, accelerating. The woman dropped her hand from her mouth, looked at him and smiled, a little embarrassed.

'Sorry,' she said, very quietly.

'It's OK.'

'Did I wake you?'

'I wasn't asleep.'

They looked at one another for a few seconds. It was, Jim Jackson thought, that moment of choice when strangers can open a conversation or politely retreat into their own worlds without offence.

'You look nervous,' he said. 'Have you not ridden a train before?'

'Once or twice,' she said. 'It's just. . . .'

She looked out of the window again, then back to him.

'Train robbers,' she said.

'Train robbers?' He felt a kick inside, as if his heart had

missed a beat then tried to catch up with itself.

'My sister was robbed on the Kansas line. They killed a man. I read in the papers that there are train robbers here in Texas, too.'

His throat was suddenly too dry to respond and in the pause she added, 'I'm being silly, aren't I?'

'No,' he said. The train was slowing again now, braking sharply. He heard the wheels complaining and he had to grip the edge of his seat. He felt his gun on his thigh. Not his gun, not the one that he had used more than ten years ago in his own train-robbing days, but the gun belonging to a Texas Ranger called Sam McRae. McRae had been the man who had arrested Jim Jackson and sent him to prison for ten years right here in Texas. Ten long years of hell. And Jim had been warned, in no uncertain terms, to never set foot in the state again.

The wheels screeched.

'What's happening?' the lady said, fear in her eyes and voice.

Jim sensed movement and when he looked across the carriage and out the far window he saw a masked rider racing alongside the train.

'They're going to rob us, aren't they?' she said.

Further up the carriage people were twisting in their seats trying to see what was occurring. There were only a half dozen other people in the carriage – two men in smart suits, a woman with a young boy and a baby, and another man, like Jim Jackson, dressed in trail clothes.

The train stopped.

From somewhere up ahead a gunshot echoed out, loud and clear, and as sharp as an Indian knife.

'They're going to rob us,' she said again. Along the carriage the baby started crying.

Jim Jackson loosened his gun in his holster.

'Take it easy,' he said. He stood up and moved across the

carriage from where he'd been sitting. He pressed himself up against the carriage bulkhead so anyone coming in mightn't see him for a second. It wasn't much, that second, but it would be enough. The way they'd used to do it was all about surprise and shock, burst into the carriage, wave a gun to scare everyone, and then work the passengers, taking what you could carry: money, purses, jewellery, watches. It had been lucrative. It had also sent him to hell for ten years.

Somebody shouted in the carriage next to theirs. He couldn't distinguish the words but there was a threat in the tone.

He heard boot-steps on the roof. Someone was running along the length of the carriage above them.

Another gunshot rang out, this one closer but still in the next carriage. Somebody screamed. He couldn't tell if it was through fear or pain.

He heard footsteps just the other side of their carriage door. A man slid open the door quickly and hard. It smashed into its stop with a sound not unlike a gunshot.

The man stepped into the carriage. His face was hidden beneath a red neckerchief, and a brown hat was pulled low over his eyes. He wore a black coat despite it being a warm day. He wasn't tall, but he was lean. He held a Colt .45 out in front of him, and he locked eyes on the woman who had been sitting opposite Jim.

'Nobody move,' he yelled. 'I damn well mean it. You move and you're dead.'

The man looked down the carriage to where one of the businessmen was rising, his hands already halfway in the air. The baby was still crying and his older brother was struggling to catch his breath too. The man in trail clothes down that end of the carriage hadn't moved but he was looking towards the train robber.

The robber sensed Jim standing right beside him.

He turned, opening his mouth to bark out another order. Jim hit him hard on the temple with the butt of his gun and the man's legs buckled and he folded to the floor. An arc of blood sprayed across the carriage.

The woman with the children started screaming. The businessman with his hands in the air was saying 'Dear God,' over and over. The woman who had been sat opposite him was staring wide-eyed at Jim. There was a splash of blood on her cheek.

At the far end of the carriage the door opened.

The man who had run along the roof of the carriage had a yellow bandana covering his face. His hat was black and he wore a light brown jacket and blue trousers. He had leather chaps over the top of his trousers and the spurs on his boots jingled as he stepped into the carriage. He had a gun in his hand.

Maybe, Jim Jackson thought, the trail-hand down that end of the carriage had seen what Jim had done and figured he ought to do something similar. For no sooner had the train robber stepped into the carriage than the trail-hand was rising, reaching for his own gun.

'Stop!' Jim yelled. You couldn't out-draw a man who already had a gun in his hand. The train robber fired twice. The roar of the gun was deafening in the carriage. The trail-hand was blown backwards. He flipped over the rear of the seat from which he had just risen.

Jim had been holding his own gun the wrong way, a grip that had allowed him to knock out the first train robber with the butt, rather than shooting him. Had the second robber chosen to shoot Jim before that trail-hand then it might have been a fatal mistake on Jim's part to have knocked out that first man rather than shoot him. It was a trait, this penchant for mercy, which had got him into trouble before. As the trail-hand landed, moaning on the carriage floor, the robber turned his attention to Jim. But those few seconds had been enough; Jim had readjusted his hold on his own gun and now he fired twice. The bullets hit the robber in the chest, smashing him backwards through the still open door.

Jim stepped away from the carriage bulkhead, ears ringing, the smell of cordite and gunpowder in the air. He turned and looked into the next carriage. The end-door to that carriage door was closed, and the blind on the window was down. Whoever was in there would have heard the shots but wouldn't know what was happening. Jim crouched down and turned over the first train robber. The man was unconscious. Jim strode along the carriage aisle, ignoring the businessmen and the crying children with their white-faced mother. He knelt alongside the cowboy that the second robber had shot. The man would live. One of the train robber's bullets had taken him in the shoulder, the other in the upper arm.

'You,' Jim Jackson said to the nearest businessman. 'Quickly.' The man looked in shock, his face pale and his lips quivering, but he stood shakily and came across to Jim.

'You have to stop the bleeding,' Jim said. 'Find some cloth. Keep it pressed hard against the wounds.' He looked up. The woman at the far end of the carriage was staring. The one with the children, too. 'The ladies will help.'

'You,' he said to the second businessman, whose mouth was moving as if he was still praying. 'Take your belt and tie up that fellow down there.' He pointed back along the carriage towards the unconscious first robber. 'Tie his arms. Take your friend's belt and tie his legs, too.'

Without waiting for the businessmen to respond, Jim went quickly to the robber he had shot.

The man was laying half in and half out of the carriage door. He was dead.

Jim felt his heart lurch again. They – Jim and his fellow train robbers back in the day – had never been violent men. In fact he had been known as Gentleman Jim Jackson. They had made a fortune whilst rarely firing a shot. It had been the early days of train robbery and people were less prepared for it, less likely to resist. But who was to say these men had been violent men? Maybe they'd were just shouting and waving guns trying to frighten people, the way Jim's gang used to, and now one was out cold and the other was dead. All because a fellow who wasn't scared of shouting and guns had been travelling in the carriage.

But this wasn't the time for deep thinking. Jim knew how these things worked. There would be two men in the next carriage along, maybe the one beyond that as well. There would be a man with a gun on the driver and engineer.

And none of them would take kindly to discovering that one of their own was dead. Once you started something you had to finish it.

He reloaded his gun as he walked back along the aisle and opened the door to the connected carriage.

Someone was bleeding on the floor. Gut-shot. A young man, maybe twenty years of age. He was squirming and moaning in pain.

There were two robbers, again with faces masked and hats pulled low. One had a gun in his hand and the other was holding a sack into which a lady and a gentleman were just dropping their purses and watches.

The robbers looked at Jim. Their eyes met. The one with the gun was raising his hand, finger tightening on the trigger, when Jim shot him. Jim's bullet took the man in the throat and he fell backwards on to a fellow in a smart black suit, white shirt, and a bootlace tie.

The one holding the sack paused, dropped the sack and raised his hands.

Jim walked towards him, keeping his eyes locked on the man, his gun steady in front of him. Peripheral vision showed a couple of young, strong-looking farmhands just beyond the man.

'Boys,' Jim said. 'Figure you can hold this one down a while?'

The boys smiled.

Jim took the man's gun from his holster. One of the farm boys grabbed the man's raised arms and yanked them down so hard behind his back that something snapped with a loud crack. The man screamed.

'Take my darn money, would you?' the boy said, and twisted the man's arms so he had no choice but to lie face down on the floor.

The far carriage door slid open.

Another train robber stood there, this one wearing a black bandanna. The masked man took in the scene and then slid the door shut again. Jim heard the man shouting, his voice become quieter almost immediately as, Jim figured, he jumped from the train.

Jim ran down the carriage.

Sure enough the man was racing across the dirt to where a colleague sat guard on a chestnut mare, holding the reins of a half dozen horses. A third man appeared running from the front of the train. A moment later there was the blast of a shotgun, and that third man went down screaming. But he scrambled to his feet again, his clothes peppered and shredded, and he made it to the horses.

The men mounted the horses, jabbed spurs into horseflesh, and then they were gone, empty-handed, wounded, and frightened, heading towards the tree line.

CHAPTER TWO

Jim Jackson led his horse down the boxcar ramp and on to the dirt alongside the railroad track. He rubbed her nose and said, 'So much for a quiet journey.' The shaking that had wracked his body following the shooting – and the killings – had stopped, but he still felt empty and sick. It hadn't been so long ago that he had killed a man for the very first time. Since then there had been others. And although it was always they – the ones he had killed – who had initiated their own demise, it didn't make the act any easier. He took a deep breath and turned around, intending to get his bearings, his first proper view of Austin. Instead he found three men standing facing him.

'This is the fellow,' Frank Stokes said. 'Daniel Flanders. He's the one.'

Frank Stokes was the train driver. Back along the track, when the train was still stationary after the attempted robbery, Jim had jumped down off the carriage at about the same time as Stokes. There had been a guard, too, and the fireman. A couple of passengers had joined them. All had stood there in the Texas heat, looking out at the trees into which the outlaws had fled, talking and trying to make sense of what had just happened. Smoke and steam had been blowing back over them and the sound of someone cursing came from inside the closest carriage. One of the passengers had told Stokes how it had been Jackson who had foiled the robbery, and when Stokes asked Jackson his name 'Daniel Flanders' had been the best that Jackson had been able to come up with. Not long before, back in New Mexico, he had been reading Daniel Defoe's Moll Flanders to a blind man who'd had his eyelids cut off by the Apache.

One of the three men standing in front of him now was wearing a black suit with a vest and a gold watch chain running from a button into a pocket. He wore wire-framed spectacles and had very little hair.

He held his hand out.

'We owe you a debt of gratitude, Mr Flanders,' the man said. 'We being the Houston and Texas Central Railroad, the passengers that ride on her, and the state of Texas itself. My name is Maxwell Higgs. I run this station. This is Charlie Entwhistle,' Maxwell indicated the man on his left. 'He's our Passenger Manager. You've met Frank, I know.'

Jim shook hands with Higgs and Entwhistle.

Over their shoulders he saw the two young country boys manhandling the captured robber off the train. The man was swearing and moaning in equal measures. Standing back, just alongside the tracks, waiting for the two boys and the robber was a fellow in a white shirt and grey vest with a gun at his hip and a star on his chest.

'I was just doing what any man would do,' Jim said.

From a carriage further along Jim saw the woman he had been sitting opposite climb out of the train – she came out backwards, and she was talking to someone who was following her. A moment later the two businessmen, looking hot and dishevelled, appeared. They were carrying the trail-hand who had been shot. The trail-hand wasn't making a sound.

'I don't think so,' Higgs said. 'You were very brave. Not many men would have done what you did. In fact we need more men like you. Yes sir, indeed. It's something to think about.'

'Like lightning, that's what they said,' Frank Stokes said. 'The ones that saw him said he drew that Colt like lightning.'

'There you go,' Higgs said. 'I'm already thinking about something for a man like you. I have an idea brewing.'

'That's as may be,' Jim said, knowing that it wasn't true; people just recalled what they wanted to recall rather than the truth. He hadn't had to draw his gun. He'd had it ready in his hand. 'But there's a couple of fellows along there have got a man needs looking after badly.' He nodded towards the businessmen. As he did so he saw the woman glance in his direction. She smiled, but it was a thin smile, as if her world had turned into something that she had never imagined. 'There may be another one on the train, too. They need a doctor. And there's two fellows need arresting and two more needs burying.'

'The doctor is on his way. The marshal's here. It's all in hand.'

'Well, I figure those folks can use all the help they can get right now. I appreciate your thanks, but please, those fellows along there need you more than I do.'

'No, no. It's all in hand, really,' Higgs said. But he did turn to Entwhistle and asked him to go and check if there was anything more he could do. He turned back to Jim. 'Now we need to thank you properly, Mr Flanders. Where are you staying?'

It wasn't something Jim had thought about yet, and he told Higgs as much.

'Well, I'd have loved to have the company put you up in the Driskell. That place was a sight to behold. You take a look up on Brazos Street. You'll be impressed. Alas, it's closed just at the moment. Prices were way too high for a town like this one. But I'll tell you what, you check into the Washington, just up from the Driskell. Tell them Maxwell Higgs sent you and that the Houston and Texas Central will collect the bill. I'll come and find you later – there are more than a few gentlemen in this town will want to shake your hand and, I suspect, there might be a job offer or two for a man like you. I mean, I didn't ask, what do you do? What brings you to Austin, Mr Flanders?'

'I'm looking for someone, that's all.'

'Well, tell me his name. I know most everybody, and if I

don't know then I know the men to ask.'

'Let's talk about that later,' Jim Jackson said.

'Yes, let's do that,' Higgs said, and held out his hand again. 'Like lightning, eh?'

The girl was in a buggy with another young woman. The two of them looked remarkably alike.

Jim Jackson nudged his horse alongside the buggy. The girl driving gave him a look worse than many a man who'd pointed a gun his way.

He held up a hand, the reins resting between his thumb and fingers, to indicate peace.

'I just wanted to check you were all right, ma'am,' he said to the girl who had been in the railway carriage with him. 'I'm sorry it happened, and I'm sorry you had to see it.'

She smiled at him.

'It's not for you to be sorry,' she said. She glanced at the woman driving the buggy. 'This is the man I was telling you about, Roberta. The one in the train.'

Roberta looked at him coldly, suspicion in her eyes.

He said, 'I wished I could've been there in Kansas.'

She opened her mouth to say something, but then snapped it shut. She said, 'How did you know—'

'You two look so alike. I figured you were sisters. Your sister here – I'm sorry, I don't think I ever got your name?'

'Rosalie,' she said. Her smile was warmer than her sister's, and now had less of the strain that had been showing when she had descended from the train a few minutes earlier.

'Rosalie told me you had been robbed on a train.'

'Yes . . . It doesn't feel safe anywhere anymore.'

'Well, I'm glad you're both OK.'

'I didn't get your name,' Rosalie said.

He smiled at her and said, 'Jim Jackson'.

It didn't occur to him to lie to her the way he had lied to Frank Stokes earlier.

'Well, thank you, Jim Jackson,' she said. Her sister flicked the buggy reins and they moved off.

Jim watched them go and then he lightly pressed his heels into his horse's flanks and followed them slowly, deeper into Austin.

It was a cow town. But it was bigger and wider and it had more squares and more streets crossing more avenues than any cow town he had ever seen before. It had more white picket fences, too. That was the first thing that grabbed him, once he had ridden past the cattle compounds and the corrals around the railway station and started heading into town. The log fences gave way to picket fences, and beyond them were more picket fences. Always white, too. The buildings behind the picket fences were neat, and most had wide porches, grass and trees in the yards. Further ahead, in the distance on a slight rise, he could see a huge construction project taking place. There were cranes, great wooden and metal beasts, and he determined to take a closer look later. He rode deeper into town and the wooden houses gave way to brick, and they started to grow additional stories. There was a church on a corner (Saint David's, according to the sign) that was more impressive than any building he had seen in a dozen years. It had towers; parts of it looked like a castle and other parts looked like a great cathedral from Europe.

He passed numerous stables and saloons. There were telegraph poles and wires strung alongside several of the streets. Horses grazed in some squares, pretty women with children ate their evening picnics in others. He rode randomly, turning left and right, not worried about getting lost as he had nowhere in mind to go. At one point he came across several fire blackened buildings and a little further on, not far from where the mighty new building was being constructed, he came across the charred remains of another great building – this one no longer so fine. Pillars still stood, but much of the building that they had once fronted was burned out or knocked down.

Further on were more saloons and stores and hotels and barbers and he was sure he'd passed more than one sheriff's office. The boardwalks were crowded towards the centre of town where the majority of saloons were located. He heard piano music and laughter, people shouting and singing. In the street were horses and wagons, dogs and water troughs. Boxes and barrels and cases were piled high on the boardwalks. The smell of smoke and cooking meat reminded him that he hadn't eaten for a while.

He turned a corner and discovered the Driscoll Hotel. The junction it lorded over was bigger than any corner he could recall. Even back in his eastern days when he had walked the prettiest and richest girl in town along the widest avenues of Clark County, Illinois, there'd been nothing like this. He wondered what Jennifer-Anne would have made of Austin, Texas. She'd have liked it, he figured. Although it was just a cow town it had a little class to it. But maybe not enough class, he thought, looking up at the Driscoll. Despite the ornamental roof and the towers and the vast balconies, the doors were closed and the windows shuttered. It was bigger than the church that had impressed him so much a few minutes earlier and it filled a whole block. Yet it looked sad, dusty and empty, as if it had been a little too ambitious for the town where it had been built.

He wondered if he'd ever see Jennifer-Anne again – she was the reason he'd come west. You couldn't marry the richest girl in Clark County unless you had some money yourself. *She'd* insisted that money didn't matter, but deep down he knew that her father and indeed her whole family would have disowned her had she married a nobody like him. He hadn't wanted her to suffer that way. So he'd asked Jennifer to give him a year and he'd headed west. He was going to make his fortune. Instead he ended up in hell.

He pushed the thoughts from his mind. He'd long trained himself not to think of Jennifer. It was the only way to survive.

Higgs had told him the Washington Hotel was just along from the Driscoll. So he turned and took a different street. The sun was getting lower now, casting long shadows. He'd find a stable, then a hotel and then a steak. In that order. But he wouldn't go near the Washington Hotel. He had no intention of being found here in Texas by anyone in authority.

He'd survived hell and had come out the other side. But back in New Mexico he'd discovered that going through that suffering – ten years in the Texas convict leasing system – had not been down to his bad luck. He'd been set up. Sure, he'd been a train robber. He didn't deny that. But he never shot anyone and he always treated everyone respectfully. At his trial, when he was being sentenced for the murder of a Texas Ranger who had happened to be on the train they were robbing, one witness, a girl, had told the jury that it hadn't been the gentleman that had done the killing.

Such testimony stood for nothing. He had been sentenced to ten years in the system and it had nearly killed him. And Texas, or rather an evil prison guard called Webster T. Ellington on behalf of Texas, had sworn that if Jackson ever set foot in the state again, this time they really would kill him.

Yet here he was.

He'd been given a lead back in New Mexico about who it was that had set him up. He had a name and a place.

But before he sought revenge he had to check on his old friends. The hell he had been through . . . it was almost too much for a man to bear. If any of them were still living through it he was going to get them out. He owed them that. And together they would take that revenge.

It was here in Austin that the prison records were kept that would lead him to his old friends.

But first: stables, a hotel, and a steak.

CHAPTER THREE

In a prison lumber camp a hundred miles north of Austin, Webster T. Ellington said to a young guard who was still learning the ropes, 'You see that feller, there? The tall one.'

'The one limping,' the guard, whose name was Billy Burke, said.

Ellington said, 'That's not a limp. That's a dead man's walk.'

They were standing by the gate. The sun was setting beyond the prisoners' huts and the sky was streaked with red, orange and purple. Crickets were chirping loudly from the long grass alongside the fence. There was a faint smell of decomposition in the air – the creek on the far side of the camp was going stagnant with the lack of rain. The young guard gripped his shotgun tightly as the prisoners made their way from the washroom back to their huts.

'You going to kill him?' Billy Burke said.

'Nope. Not allowed to.'

'Not allowed to?'

Ellington spat tobacco juice on the ground.

'Nope. They want him dead, but I'm not allowed to kill him.'

Billy said, 'Sounds confusing, if you want my opinion.'

'Nope and nope,' Ellington said. 'I mean, it ain't confusing and I don't need your opinion. But he needs to die soon. Fact

20

is, if he were a black man then I'd take him out to the creek and shoot him. Tell 'em all he was running away. That would be the end of it. But that feller there, Winters is his name, he's got a family probably. There are records. You know what I mean?'

Billy nodded.

'If he dies – when he dies – it's got to be above board. There'll be an investigation, most likely. Witness statements, the lot. If he runs and I shoot him, then that'll be OK. If he catches his death working night and day, rain and shine, that'll be all right. If he gets into a fight and someone strangles him . . . You understand?'

'But none of that has happened yet?'

'Nope. And it needs to soon. See, his time is coming up.'

'He's due to be released?'

'Another six months. And I can't let it happen.'

'Why?'

'I had one in a camp way over west. Same thing.'

'What happened?'

Ellington spat on the ground. 'He got released. I got the blame.'

'The blame?'

'Yep. They demoted me. I was a captain back then. They told me he should never have been released. But that was nothing to do with me. He got ten years. He did ten years. The governor released him. But they said he should have been long dead.'

'Who are they?'

Ellington shrugged. 'Damned if I know. Government, maybe. But they had the power to strip me of my rank and send me to one rat-hole camp after another. Wife gave up on me. She's somewhere else these days. Said enough was enough. Just because he didn't have the good grace to die.'

'And you weren't allowed to kill him?'

'Now you're getting it. Sonofabitch was young. He didn't

look tough. He wasn't tough. He used to cry like a baby whenever I gave him the bat.'

'The bat?'

'I'll show you later. He used to weep for his mother. I worked him harder than any two men. He took it all. He was like a ghost when I was done. Couldn't string two words together and couldn't stop shaking. He was like a starving and whipped wet dog. But he survived and they released him, and they took it out on me. I suspect he's dead now. Can't imagine he lasted a single night outside the camp.'

'What was his name?'

'Jackson. Jim Jackson was his name.'

In the Rio Grande Steakhouse, just off Brazos Street, Maxwell Higgs forked a piece of tender, rare-done, Texas beef into his mouth, chewed a while, washed it down with red wine, and said, 'Daniel Flanders. I'll bet you five dollars to a dime that's not his real name.'

Opposite him at the table sat Ben Adams, Houston and Texas railroad trouble-shooter. Adams was a bearded man, of medium height, who always seemed to give the impression of being taller than he was. He had a team of men who would ride trains looking out for the passengers, making sure there was no trouble. The men tended to have violent backgrounds. Standing up to train robbers and bandits wasn't a job for shrinking violets. Adams himself had been a sheriff in Abilene and had tracked and killed cattle rustlers down by the border and over in San Antonio. He had a reputation as both a fist-fighter and a knife-fighter and had done a year in Huntsville for blinding a man in one eye during a fight over a card game. He was annoyed that this latest robbery had taken place on a train where he never had a man stationed.

'Why so?' Adams said. He was a man of few words, and softly spoken when he did speak – unless he became riled, when the volume of his voice never changed, but the tone became hard and sharp. Like flint, Maxwell Higgs had once remarked to a colleague when talking about Ben Adams. They'd just witnessed the softly spoken man tearing a strip off one of his men. The man was shaking afterwards, yet Adams' voice had hardly risen above a whisper.

Higgs reached down on to the floor and came up with a battered hardback book. He placed it on the table. The book had a brown cover with gold embossed writing on it.

'One of Marion's.'

'I see,' Adams said.

'Daniel Defoe. Moll Flanders,' Higgs said. 'You're not telling me that was a coincidence?'

'I'm not telling you anything. You're telling me. A lot of folks call themselves by made-up names,' Adams said. 'In fact I'd say more than half of the folks I come into contact with are known by something other than their birth name.'

'And the people you come into contact generally have a reason for not wanting folks to know who they really are.'

Higgs ate another chunk of steak and sipped some more wine.

'You think he's hiding something?' Adams asked.

'I know he's hiding something. The fellow was a hero. He could be basking in glory. But instead of that he's giving us a false name and has disappeared.'

'Disappeared?'

'Bet you another five dollars to a dime that if we walk down to the Washington after we've finished up here he won't have booked in there. I told him the Railroad would pay. Why would a man turn down a free hotel room for as long as he's here?'

'Maybe you're wrong.'

'Maybe I am. But we can check it out later. He was as fast as lightning, too. That's what they said.'

'A gunman.'

'Uh-huh.'

'Doesn't mean to say he's here to do something wrong.'

'Nope. All I'm saying, the reason I called you over here, is that I figure something's up with the fellow. Figured you might be interested.'

'Oh I am. And I thank you.'

'You'll look into it?'

Adams nodded, then lifted his own glass and drank. He wiped his lips. 'Tell me again what this Defoe fellow looks like.'

Fifty miles west of Austin, Texas, a small farmhouse stood at the edge of a copse of live oaks. The farmhouse faced several acres that hadn't been worked in years and were getting swallowed by tangled weeds and grass. At the farmhouse window, dirty with dust and grease, Red Kelly drank whiskey straight from the bottle, stared at the distant prairie, and swore again.

'Son of a bitch killed Little Joe,' he said.

'We don't know that,' Callum Short said. Callum had been the one holding the horses over by the tree line when the train robbery had taken place.

'I heard shooting inside the carriage along from where I was. Four shots, I swear. That fellow I saw, the tall one with the gun, he had that look in his eyes. Ringo was dead. I saw him on the floor. He'd been shot in the face. That fellow, I should have shot him, but some boys and Wes was between him and me.' Red took another long drink of whiskey. 'Sonofabitch.'

'I should have shot that damn engineer,' Ned Donovan said. He was across the room by another window. His trousers were off and he was picking tiny shards of lead from the back of his left thigh. 'You try and do the right thing – let a fellow live – and he peppers you with lead.'

'Might be that Little Joe got captured alive,' Callum said. 'Wes was.'

'Yeah, maybe,' Red said. 'I just got a feeling that's all. Can't see how that fellow would have been in my carriage if Joe and Lech were still alive.' He finished the whiskey, looked at the empty bottle and threw it across the room. 'We need to know for sure.'

'We going to Austin?' Callum said.

'Well, we certainly ain't robbing no more trains. Not with just three of us,' Red said. He looked across at Ned. 'Stop picking at your scabs, Ned, and get your pants back on. If my brother's alive, we have to bust him out of wherever he is before they hang him. If he's dead we got a feller to kill to make up for it.'

CHAPTER FOUR

Jim Jackson breathed in the cool morning air. It tasted good. Not just clean, but cleansing.

Yesterday he had killed two men. He hadn't thought he would sleep a wink, and yet he had slept well. He couldn't help but wonder what that said about him, about the man he had become.

He stood outside the Alamo Hotel and looked left and right. The reason he had come here, the reason he had been on that train, was somewhere in this town was a place where the Penitentiary Board kept all of their records. Hell, somewhere in this town was where Texas kept all of its records on everything. The question was: where?

He watched two girls walk by – no more than twenty years old, at a guess. They both had books in their hands, smiles on their faces, and a carefree jaunt in the way they walked. Across from the hotel was a square with trees growing in it and mown grass around the roots. A buggy, not unlike the one that Rosalie's sister Roberta had been driving yesterday, crossed his vision. The buggy was clean and painted black with gold coach-lines. The paintwork shone as if it had been polished to within an inch of its life. The horse pulling the buggy was a grey, well groomed, well fed, and it held its head up as if it knew it was pulling a fine cart in a fine city. It all felt a thousand miles away from the world he had come from, where not

26

so long ago he had stood in a sun-drenched street in a New Mexico border town and had killed a man in a gunfight whilst drunken people roared and cheered. The killing had been a turning a point in his life. That terrible act – an act that had been forced upon him – had hauled him up from the darkness that had enveloped him as a result of his experiences here in Texas and brought him back into a light that enabled him to live again, and ultimately to arrive here, in this very different Texas.

He walked slowly towards the livery stables, smiling at people, nodding good morning. It was like being back in Illinois. It was civilised. It reminded him of how wild things had been – and still were – if you just headed west for a few days, maybe even just a few hours.

He became conscious of the gun on his hip. Back in New Mexico you were the odd one out if you didn't have a gun. Here a few people were looking at him as if he was some kind of savage. He smiled more widely at those people.

At the stables his horse nuzzled up against him. She was well fed and watered, and the stall was clean. He told her he'd be back later, that he had no intention of staying here any longer than he could. Though even as he said the words he wondered about them. This civilised living . . . it reminded him of home. If indeed he still had a home. All the wildness, the savagery; was that really him? he wondered.

'Happy' Harry Harvey, the scowling owner of the livery, was in his office when Jim knocked on the door and pushed it open. Happy was counting money and writing numbers in a ledger. He had a thin black cheroot gripped in his teeth and the smoke curled upwards, gathered at the ceiling, and started spreading out. To Jim, it smelled like someone had set fire to an outhouse.

'Yep?' Happy said, before he'd even looked up. 'What is it?' He looked up. 'Ah, yours is the mare. Fine horse. You want to sell her?'

'Nope.'

'Pity. You want another night?'

'Maybe. I'll let you know later. She looks happy. Thank you.'

'Best livery in Austin. What can I do for you?' He spoke and breathed and puffed smoke all whilst keeping the cheroot clamped in his teeth.

'You know where in town I might get information?'

'What kind of information?'

'Prison information. I'm looking for my brother. He's locked up somewhere in Texas. I was told if I came to Austin all the records are here.'

'Well they ain't in this office.'

'Damn, I thought they would be.'

Happy stared at him. Smoked seeped from the sides of the man's mouth. For a moment the smoke made it look as if he was smiling. Maybe he was, Jim thought. Maybe that's as close as he ever gets.

'What did your brother do?'

'He robbed a train.'

'There's a lot of it about. Surprised they didn't hang him. The railroad companies don't take kindly to such things. Much of the time these days they don't even get to court, know what I mean? Fellow over at the railroad likes to shoot 'em whilst they're running, I heard.'

'You know where in town I might need to go?'

'For information? Well, I'd have said the Capitol building. They had all the records there. But the place burned down a few years back and they haven't built the new one yet.'

'That's the one that's going up now?'

'Something to see, ain't it? How long's your brother been in prison?'

'Ten years.'

Happy looked through the smoke. 'And you're only just looking for him now?'

'Uh-huh.'

Happy stared at him for a moment. Now he really did smile as if he was seeing inside Jim's head.

'Wasn't a family concern by any chance, this train-robbing, was it?'

Jim said nothing, but he did allow himself to return Happy's smile.

'I wouldn't be surprised if the paperwork you're after didn't go up in flames,' Happy said. 'A lot of it did. You should have seen the fire. They were throwing buckets of water on it from the front whilst carrying boxes of paper and paintings and all sorts out the back. You know we have a fire department in town?'

'No, I didn't know that.'

'Lot of good it did them, the fire department. The building's on a hill and there wasn't any way to pump water up there.'

'So where's the government building now?'

'They have a bunch of offices up on Capitol Avenue, or Capitol Drive, whatever they're currently calling it. Have a wander up there. You can't miss them. Ask one of the pretty ladies or the men in suits. Up there they all work for the state.'

'I appreciate it.'

'I hope you find your brother.'

'Me too.'

He saw her before she saw him. She was walking along the front of a large building just down the street from the construction work. She was wearing her bonnet – which is how he recognized her – and appeared to be reading the plaques besides the many doors on the building. About a dozen feet away from him she paused, smiled to herself as if she'd found the building she wanted. Then she noticed him. She jumped in surprise, and smiled again.

'Mr Jackson.'

'*Jim*, please. How are you, Rosalie? I'm sorry; I never got your surname. I trust Rosalie isn't too informal?'

'No, no. It's fine. It's Rosalie Robertson, by the way.'

'Well, Miss Robertson, what brings you here on this fine morning?'

'A job,' she said. 'Hopefully.'

'A job?' He was genuinely surprised. Interested, too. It had never occurred to him that such a pretty woman, with such fine clothes, and such a way of holding herself would be in need of work.

'We've all got to make a living.'

'I guess so.'

'My sister—'

'Roberta.'

'Yes. She's a clerk here in Austin. She said there were jobs going and that's why I came to town. It's worth a try. There's nothing back west. Nothing I care for anyway.'

Suddenly there was a whole host of questions he wanted to ask her. *Back west.* Where was she from? What had she been doing out there? Right now, the way the low morning sun was shining on her face reminded him of the way she had looked when he had first seen her on the train the previous day.

'What's this building? What's the job?'

'It's the Centre for Population and Housing. They're preparing for another census, so Roberta says. It takes a few years.'

'And Roberta works here?'

'Yes.'

He looked up and down the street. There were dozens of buildings, seemingly hundreds of people.

'What is it?' she said.

'The reason I'm here. I'm trying to find out about some friends. I have no idea where to go.'

'You think Roberta could help?'

'I just need a pointer.'

'I can ask her.'

'Would you?'

'Of course.' She smiled. 'After what you did for . . . all of us. I mean, are you OK? I never asked yesterday.'

'I'm fine. I won't say it was nothing, but I'm OK.'

'What are they going to do? Are you going to get a reward? Will you have to go to court for their trial? The ones you didn't. . . .'

'I don't know yet. I imagine so – regarding the court. I doubt there'll be any reward.'

'There darn well ought to be.'

He smiled. He liked the way she swore on his behalf. He wanted to tell her that he wasn't planning on staying in Austin long enough to have any involvement at all in the aftermath of the train robbery, but he held his tongue.

'So, who are your friends?'

He looked at her, held her gaze. He wasn't sure if she didn't blush slightly. 'You may think less of me when I tell you.'

'I would never think less of you.'

'You don't know me.'

'I think I do.'

'There are five of them.'

'OK. I'm good with names.'

'You don't need to write them down?'

'I'm good with names. My sister says I'm perfect for this job.'

'OK. Hans Freidlich—'

'How do you spell that?'

He spelled it out.

'Next one.'

'Leon Winters.'

'OK.'

'John Allan. That's Allan with an A. I mean, not at the start but at the end. Well it starts with an A as well.'

'I know what you meant.' The edges of her eyes crinkled when she smiled. 'Next.'

31

Patrick Reagan. And William Moore.'

She repeated all the names.

'Did I get them right?'

'Yep.'

She repeated them again.

'And these men,' she said. 'Your friends. You want to know where they are.'

'Yep.'

'Would they have completed the last census?' There was a glint of humour in her eyes.

'I doubt it. They're all in prison.'

'You?' she said.

'I was, too,' he said. He knew that when she started digging – or when her sister started digging – they would find out what these men had once been. And, by connection, what he had been.

'I'm a good man,' he added. 'Even back then, I was a good man. You know, they used to call me the Gentleman Train Robber.'

It was as if the whole street had disappeared and only the two of them remained. She was looking into his eyes and for a moment he thought she was going to throw the names back in his face – metaphorically – and declare him as bad as the men on the train, as bad as the men that had robbed her sister previously, and had caused so much fear in their lives. But she didn't. She held his gaze and he could almost see her mind working, trying to figure out this man who had saved her, and others, who had risked his life for them.

She said, 'I have to admit you're an intriguing man, Mr Jackson.'

'Jim, please.'

'I think Mr Jackson suits the moment better.'

'Do you now think less of me?'

'I knew from the very first moment I saw you that you weren't an office clerk.'

'Will you see if you can locate my friends?'

'There's a steakhouse along the road they say is divine. It's Lansdale's Steakhouse. How about I meet you there at seven o'clock this evening?'

'I'll be there.'

'Now if you'll excuse me, I have an interview to go to.'

'Thank you, Rosalie. Good luck with the interview.'

She smiled and turned away, but as she did so he heard her whispering the names of his old friends quietly.

Ben Adams stood on the corner of Brazos Street. It was a beautiful morning. Fresh clean air, a good clear sky, and an easy feeling in his bones. The sort of morning it would be nice to be sitting quietly in a carriage on a train heading west when some young kid figured train robbery an easy way to make some money. Adams let his right hand rest on the Colt strapped to his thigh. Dead or alive, it was always good to bring in a train robber. Kept the passengers – both current and future – happy and, more importantly made the likes of Maxwell Higgs realize just how vital it was to employ someone such as Adams. It had been a bit quiet recently and the fact that he and his men had missed that robbery yesterday, well, that was the only cloud on the horizon of this otherwise fine day. At least this Daniel Flanders – whoever he was – had been there.

Today's job was to find Flanders.

Higgs had been right – the man hadn't spent the night in the Washington Hotel despite the offer of free bed and board. No one matching his description had even been in the Washington. It wasn't a surprise. Indeed, Adams felt the muscles in his shoulders and neck twist and turn and tighten. It was as if God was telling him to be careful, that there might be more to Flanders than either he or Higgs knew.

Adams pulled a pouch from his pocket and started making up a cigarette. He kept one eye on the Washington Hotel across the street. Not because he expected Flanders to turn up there, but just because it was a main street and there were a lot of folks walking by and per chance he might see a tall man, handsome, with a dark beard – not too long – with grey in it, a blue jacket that wouldn't be any good in a rainstorm or winter, and a dark brown hat. The fellow would have bright blue eyes, a Colt on his right hip, black boots with spurs, and a fine-looking grey mare. That was how Higgs had described Daniel Flanders, and you never knew when you might get lucky and just see the feller walking by. Even in a town the size of Austin it could happen.

By the time he had finished his smoke, no one of Flanders' description had walked by. It looked like it was going to have to be him that did the walking. The grey mare was the key. There were what, ten, livery stables in town now? Or was it eleven? Hell, that might even be some that he didn't know about; the place was growing so quickly. But it was a safe bet that Flanders' grey mare was in one of them.

Time to start walking.

CHAPTER FIVE

The two dead men were strapped to boards in a room at the Houston and Texas Central Railroad station building. The boards were propped upright against one wall, and a dozen bricks had been placed against the bottom of each plank to prevent them sliding down. The room had windows along one side and the midday sun shone through, catching the dust motes in the air and making it appear as if lights were being shone on the dead men. Both men had been stripped to the waist. They had sunken chests, thin arms, and white skin. The one on the left had two bullets hole in his chest. The one on the right a single bullet hole in his throat. There was no blood on the bodies and the men's eyes were closed.

'They look like they're sleeping,' a boy said.

'The big sleep,' someone said from behind him.

A grey-haired woman added, 'There's no sleep to be had where those fellows have gone.'

The Railroad had invited everyone to view the bodies. 'See what happens to folks who think they can rob the customers of the Houston and Central,' Maxwell Higgs had said over and over again as the queues formed at the station.

A photographer was setting up his camera and magnesium flash pan in front of the two corpses, and Higgs had a couple of employees hold everyone else back to allow him to get a clear and steady shot. The queue grew so it stretched out of the station building. The photographer took his shots and, with the magnesium smoke still hanging in the air, Higgs then allowed people to go right up close and gaze at the bodies.

'Take a good look,' he said. 'We at the Houston and Central have your safety at heart. We have men on every train protecting you from bandits like these. Come on. Take a good look. And son,' he looked at the boy who had made the sleeping remark, 'you study hard and get yourself a good job one day. Maybe right here at the railroad. Don't ever think of becoming a train robber. No sir.'

Red Kelly, his eyes bloodshot from riding through the night, his coat and hat and boots dusty for the same reason, stood in the doorway and said to Callum Short, 'They killed Little Joe.'

'I can see him.'

Red turned to go. 'I don't need to see no more.'

Callum caught his arm. He whispered, 'You need to pay your respects. You'll regret it if you don't.'

Red stared at him. He pulled his arm away from Callum's grip, but he stayed in the queue.

'Ringo, too,' Ned Donovan said. He appeared even more tired than Red. The ride through the night from their farmhouse to Austin had been just as painful as actually getting shot in the butt. He'd ridden standing in his stirrups for as long as he could. When his calf and thigh muscles complained too much he'd sit down and then all the shotgun pellet wounds started complaining even louder. So he'd stand up again. Over and over. Up and down.

Callum said 'I guess the fact they ain't here means Wes and Lech ain't dead.'

The queue shuffled forward.

'Guess so,' Red said quietly. He was watching the fellow in charge, a bald-headed man in spectacles and a suit. The man was spouting off about how safety was the railroad's number one concern.

'Excuse me, mister,' Red said, louder now, catching the suited fellow's attention.

'Yes, sir?'

'Who shot 'em? I mean I appreciate you keeping us safe. I'd like to shake the feller's hand who shot these two.'

Maxwell Higgs smiled. 'Thank you. Yes, we do strive to keep you safe. The man who shot them? We have guards on every train. You wouldn't spot them. But they're there.'

'And this was one of your guards?'

'Yes indeed.'

'I'd sure like to shake his hand.'

'I'll pass on your appreciation, sir. I'm sure you understand that we can't reveal the identity of our guards.'

'Thank you, Mister. . . ?'

'Higgs. Maxwell Higgs. No thank *you*, sir.'

The queue shuffled forwards, and a few moments later Red Kelly was standing right in front of the body of his dead brother. 'Don't worry, kid,' he mouthed. 'Folks is going to pay.'

Happy Harvey's wife was a fiery red-haired Irish woman named Caroline. He told anyone who listened – always making sure that Caroline wasn't in hearing distance, and always prefacing his statement with 'Don't tell her I said this, but' – that the reason he spent so much time at the livery was that even the wildest, most badly behaved, angry, and stubborn stallion was a darn sight easier to figure out and control than his wife. Yet whenever he said such things it always came back to bite him. Even if his confidantes never uttered a word it was as if she somehow knew. *Karma*, she'd say. *It's karma.* Many a time she tried to explain to him what this mysterious magic was.

Here it was in action.

Only this morning he'd mentioned to that stranger with the grey mare that there was a feller down at the railroad liked to shoot train robbers under the pretext that they were running away, rather than go through the rigmarole (and possibility of acquittal) that came with taking them to trial. Now that fellow had walked through his door.

Happy took a deep pull on his cheroot. That was another reason for the long hours at the stables: Caroline wouldn't let him smoke them at home. She said they smelled like the Devil was burning a trail-hand's socks down in Hell.

He angled his head towards the ceiling, breathed out a stream of smoke, and said 'How can I help you?' He couldn't remember the fellow's name, but decided he wouldn't have used it even if he could remember.

'I'm looking for someone.' The man's voice was quiet.

'All I got here are horses.'

'Funny,' the man said.

'Not being funny. Just saying it as it is.'

'The fellow I'm looking for has stabled up a grey mare.'

Happy thought back to his visitor earlier that morning, the train robber. Or at least that's what he had assumed the fellow had been. He had seemed like a good man. But here was . . . *Adams* – that was his name. Here was Adams asking after the feller, and word was you didn't want to mess with Adams.

'A grey mare?'

'Yep. Came in last night.'

Happy pursed his lips. He wanted to say *nope, no grey mares here, mister*, for no other reason than he'd liked the feller this morning. But there was growing knot in the pit of his belly. He recalled someone over at the Buffalo Bar telling him once how Adams had broken a man's fingers one by one until the man revealed the whereabouts of a cowboy that this Adams was after. The chap said that Adams had done three fingers before the man had given up the information. Another man at the bar said that the feller had given up the information after just one finger had been broken, but that Adams had done two more just for fun, or rather because the man hadn't offered up the information right away.

'Yes,' Happy said, not feeling good about it. 'I do have a grey mare here. And yes, he came in last night.'

He breathed in smoke but it burned his throat and made him cough. He placed the cheroot into a cup of cold coffee on his desk. It sizzled. A moment later Happy realized he was clasping his fingers together as if to protect them.

'Fellow give you his name?'

'Nope.'

'What did he look like?'

'Tall. Had a beard. Going grey.' No point in lying.

'Say when he'd be back?'

'Said he might be leaving today, or might want another night.'

'Did he say anything else? Where he was staying? Where he was going?'

The thing was Adams could check on the horse. He could walk out back and see the horse for himself. Sure there were many more grey mares than one, but it hadn't been worth the risk to deny that the feller had come here. But now Happy was feeling bad, feeling like he'd given the tall man up. There was a different knot in his stomach now – a knot of disappointment in himself.

'No,' Happy said, hoping his voice sounded stronger than it felt. 'Never said nothing.'

Adams' eyes were the colour of gunmetal. They were as hard as gunmetal too. For a second Happy thought that Adams was going to call his lie and then break all of his fingers. He fumbled for another cheroot whilst his fingers were good for it.

'I'm going to send a man over. He'll be here in fifteen minutes. If this fellow comes back before then you keep him talking. You do that?'

'Sure.'

Happy flicked a Lucifer into life. He applied the flame to his fresh cigarette.

'And another thing.'

'Yes?'

'Those cigarettes stink. Next time I come in, if you're smoking one, you put it out. If you're not smoking one, you don't start.'

CHAPTER SIX

She had green eyes. He hadn't noticed this before. The previous times they had met, her bonnet had shielded her eyes. But this evening her hair was loose. It fell softly over her shoulders. She wore a light blue blouse, blue trousers, and black boots. The trousers and boots were clean and new looking, but she was like a different woman to the one he had met on the train and again outside the government building. She looked far more at ease, far more relaxed, but no less pretty.

'Divine,' Jim Jackson said, smiling.

She looked at him across the table.

'Divine?'

There had been a time, a long time ago, when he never thought he'd smile, laugh, or joke again.

'You. . . .' He let the word hang. It could go either way. 'You look divine,' he said.

She raised an eyebrow. 'Thank you.'

'This place, you described it as divine, too. You were right.'

'Don't spoil it,' she said, smiling also.

He raised a wine glass and she followed suit. They touched glasses.

'My sister told me off for having dinner with you on my second night in town. But then she's always telling me off about something. She came right here to Austin because the jobs were good and plentiful. I went to Kansas and then

41

Colorado. She told me off about that.'

'It sounds adventurous. You were brave.'

'I'm not brave. I wasn't alone. There was a group of us.'

'Nevertheless.'

'Well, it didn't last. I'm back now.' She paused. 'I was scared. I mean I was scared on the train. I was scared in Kansas and Colorado. Sometimes you just have to do things though, whether you're scared or not.'

'I know exactly what you mean.'

'You don't strike me as a man who'd be scared of much.'

'You might be surprised.'

A waiter appeared at their table and they ordered rare steak and vegetables.

'You know, when she discovered who you were and who your friends were Roberta almost locked me in my room.'

'But you'd have climbed out the window,' he said, joking, but her eyes widened and she told him she had been about to say that very same thing.

'Back east we used to make a wish if we said the same thing at the same time.'

'Back east?'

'Everybody started back east, didn't they?'

'I guess so,' she said. Then: 'You intrigue me, you know?'

'Really?'

'Jim Jackson. Train robber. Murderer. Convict.'

'No wonder your sister didn't want you to meet me.'

'I told her I don't see you as a murderer. She told me, in no uncertain terms, that I'd already seen you kill a man.'

'She was right.'

'But it wasn't murder. You were protecting us. I don't see you . . . I can't see you as a murderer.'

'I never murdered anyone before, either. They said I did. They framed me and my friends for it. But I didn't do it.'

She stared at him; her pretty green eyes and soft curls made him feel warm.

'I know,' she said.

They sat quietly for a few moments.

'How did it go? The interview, I mean.'

'They hired me.'

'I'm pleased.'

'I don't know. It seemed like a good idea when I was out west. Come back to a real town. Make something of myself.' She paused. 'Find a man. Raise a family.'

'It sounds nice.'

'Does it?'

'If that's what you want,' he said.

They drank more wine. The silences were good silences, not awkward, but space that allowed the thoughts and considerations room to breathe. The waiter brought their steaks and more wine. In the corner a man in a bow tie started playing very quietly on a piano.

'Your friends are dead,' she said.

He had thought they would be. His heart sank into a new emptiness.

'All but one. I'm sorry.'

'All but one?' That was something. He leant forward. 'Who?'

'I have to go through them in the order you told me – it's how I remember.'

'OK.'

'Hans Freidlich: they hanged him. They hanged him right away. Said he was the leader of the gang.'

'He was.'

'Leon Winters—'

'LT.'

'LT?'

'We called him LT. It was short for Long Tall Winters. He's over six feet tall.'

She smiled.

'He's still alive. He's the one.'

43

'Where?'

'He's in a prison camp. I wrote it down. Roberta cursed me for asking but she did it. I actually think she liked you.'

'It was a brief romance,' he said, trying to keep the moment light, but feeling his insides churning. *Leon was still alive.* One of them was still alive. It was why he had come to Austin.

She smiled and handed him a slip of carefully folded paper. The writing inside was beautifully neat. The words chilled him.

'Leasing Camp 13,' he said. 'Prairie City, Madison County.'

'It's about a hundred miles north of here. Are you OK? Your hand is shaking.'

He put the note down and clasped his fingers together. Back when he was just out of a leasing camp he had been known as Trembles. That's what they did to you. They took everything from you and left you worthless, with nothing but fear coursing through your body every second of every day.

'He's still there,' he said, almost to himself.

'Are you sure you're all right?'

He took a long drink of wine. Wine and whiskey had been how, in the old days, he had taken care of those trembles. He had drunk so much that the nervousness was erased by alcohol. The trouble was, everything else – dignity, honesty, pride, hours of the day and night – were erased too. It had been a tough price to pay. This wine . . . it had been a risk to drink again. Would he slide backwards into something he had worked so hard to escape from? But he felt that the moment, the evening, with Rosalie had warranted it. So he had taken the risk.

'I'm fine,' he said, wiping his mouth.

'You want the others?' she said.

'Yes, please.'

'John Allan, with an A: there are no records.'

'No records?'

'None.'

'Patrick Reagan: he died in Huntsville three years back

from pneumonia. William Moore: he was shot whilst trying to escape from a chain gang.'

She leaned back in her chair.

'I'm sorry the information isn't better.'

He drank some more wine.

'No, it's good. I really appreciate it. Please thank your sister for me.'

'Can you tell me about it?' she said. 'You did ten years, my sister said. Camp Number Five. I can see from your reaction that it wasn't good.'

He shook his head. 'Trust me, it's not a story for this evening.' He wanted to say it wasn't a story for a pretty woman, someone so pure and innocent, so clean.

She looked at him. There was a sheen of wetness in her eyes as if she was holding back tears for him, and the story he was afraid to tell her.

'Another evening, then?' she said, blinking away those unshed tears.

The piano man launched into a soft version of an old song, 'When You and I Were Young' that he and Jennifer-Anne had once danced to a lifetime ago.

'Are you staying in Austin?' he asked. 'I don't mean now, tonight. I mean for good.'

'I've got a job. I'll be here for a while.'

'Then yes, another evening.' He smiled. She smiled back and for the first time in a long time he wanted to kiss a woman. 'But I won't lie. Tomorrow I'll be gone.'

A look of disappointment passed over her face.

'Just for a while,' he said. But the truth was, if he was successful in what he was planning to do, staying in Texas – let alone coming back to Austin – might be akin to putting his head in a noose himself. But she was pretty. And he did want to kiss her.

'LT,' she said, as if those two letters explained everything.

'LT.'

'You're a fascinating man, Jim Jackson.'

'And you're a beautiful lady, Rosalie Robertson.'

'Am I not fascinating, too?'

'I don't know. Tell me about Kansas and Colorado.'

Ben Adams sat on a stool by the bar, nursing a beer. He looked across the room, through the large archway that led into the restaurant, and watched the man supposedly called Daniel Flanders talking to a very pretty young woman.

The way it happened, his man, George Dubois, whom Adams had installed over at the livery, had been sitting quietly in the corner of the stables when Flanders had come by to check on his horse. Flanders had spoken to the horse for a while, told the mare that he had a date with a pretty girl that evening. He'd checked the horse's food and water, and told the horse that he knew she was being well looked after but that it never hurt to check. Then he'd said he'd be back, maybe first thing in the morning and had left.

George Dubois – he would do well that kid – had used his initiative and had followed Flanders.

George had waited outside the Alamo Hotel for a couple of hours in the late afternoon heat and, just about the time he was busting badly to relieve himself, one of his fellow Houston and Central guards had happened along. Dubois had collared the man to take over observation duties for a minute whilst George had done the business in an alleyway. After that he'd sent his co-worker to find Adams.

An hour later Adams arrived and had taken over the watching himself. Early evening Daniel Flanders had come out of the Alamo looking all scrubbed up, rested, and pretty jaunty.

Who wouldn't be jaunty, Adams thought now, looking at the woman, *with a lady as pretty that hanging on your every word?*

When she handed Flanders a note that made him go quite white, Adams sat upright. It looked like Flanders had seen a ghost, not a piece of paper.

Adams already had another man back up at the stables with orders not to let Flanders go anywhere. Meanwhile, Adams figured, it might be worth asking this woman what was in that note. Probably easier to ask her than Flanders. No point alerting the man to anything at this stage. After all, he might turn out to be a nobody, although the tenseness that had been in Adams' neck and shoulders all day was like some kind of warning system suggesting otherwise. And why was Flanders hiding himself away if he had nothing to hide?

No, Flanders wasn't a nobody.

But who was he? That was the question.

CHAPTER SEVEN

'I can walk from here,' Rosalie said.

'I wouldn't dream of it.'

'Austin is quite safe,' she said.

'How do you know? You only arrived yesterday.'

'My sister has told me all about it.'

'Well, I've enjoyed you company. The least I can do is to make it last as long as possible.'

That was the thing. She wanted it to last as long as possible, as well. He really was fascinating. Handsome, too. Tall and lean and rugged. Brave and fearless with a gun, and charming. But most of all he was intriguing. A self-confessed train robber who had been through some kind of hell that he wouldn't talk about, but had voluntarily returned to the scene of that hell to rescue his friends from the same fate.

And tomorrow he was leaving.

Yes, it would be nice to have five more minutes of his company, but a girl had to make her own stand once in a while. He was leaving, and for all his talk of coming back, she believed she knew what kind of man he was. He was a man of the west, not of a city like Austin. He wouldn't fit here, in an office, or even working on the construction site. That would be yet another kind of hell to him.

So it was goodbye, and no need to walk her home.

'I've enjoyed your company, too. I hope you have some

success with your friend Leon.'

'I really appreciate you getting the information.'

'Thank Roberta, not me.'

'If I walk you home perhaps I could?'

She laughed.

'I could lie and say Roberta will be asleep, but I know she'll be waiting up for me. I'll thank her for you. Now please, let me go.'

'Let you go?'

'Yes. Let me go. If you ever come back please look me up, care of the Centre for Population and Housing.'

He looked at her and she felt her heartbeat quicken. His eyes held hers.

'Let me go.' But even as she said the words she reached out her hands for him to hold.

'I'll watch you, if you insist on walking alone.'

'I'll be fine.'

She eased her hands free, turned, and walked away.

Jim Jackson sighed. It had been a long time since he had felt this way about a woman. It wasn't a physical thing – or rather, it wasn't just a physical thing. There was no denying that Rosalie was very beautiful. She held herself well, too, walked nicely, and had a poise and grace about her. So it was that. But it wasn't just that. She was her own woman, knew her own mind. Was prepared to go on a date – if that's what it had been – with a man that she had seen kill someone the day before. She had travelled to the west – like he – and though she had come back, admitting that it had scared her, the tales she had told were far from that of a fearful woman. He admired the way that she hadn't judged him. She was caring, that much was clear, too. It was all of these things, and he hadn't felt like this since he had walked away from Jennifer-Anne all those years ago in a bid to make a fortune that would be worthy of her.

He watched Rosalie now. He willed her to turn. *One more*

---

uth close to her ear. 'I have no qualms about shooting a y. I've done it before. Now keep walking.'

She twisted, trying to see him.

'Keep walking.'

He was just a shape behind her. A shape that had a very rong grip on her wrist. A shape that smelled of beer. A shape ith a harsh but quiet voice and, she hoped, a steady trigger finger.

'Cross the street.'

There was no one around. And anyway, so what if there had been?

'Who are you?' she said, trying to keep her voice steady.

'Believe it or not, I'm the good guy.'

She looked up at the moon and felt tears on her face. For all her adventures out west, adventures that had always felt scary and as if she was on the edge of great danger, there had never been anything like this.

'Left,' he said.

Together, walking closely like moonlit lovers, they circled back into the business district.

It was a warehouse, or maybe a storeroom. It was dark and it smelled damp. He lit an oil lamp and he sat her down on a chair in the middle of the room. In the flickering light she saw he was a thin man with hard eyes and a beard.

There was a table in the corner and a second chair pushed neatly beneath it. There was a coil of rope on the table. In the light from the oil lamp she thought she saw stains on the floor.

Blood.

Or maybe it was just the damp that she could smell.

Either way she shivered.

He took off his hat and placed it on the table. He ran a hand through thinning hair. He looked old, she thought. Fifty-ish.

'What was in the note?' he said.

smile, please.

But she didn't turn, and he understood why. She had felt the attraction, too. But he was going away. Leon needed his help more than he needed to stay here and fall in love.

When he was sure she wasn't going to turn, he turned instead. He'd make a start right away. Ride through the night. The sooner he could get to Madison County the sooner he could figure a way of getting Leon out of there.

Ben Adams watched the two of them hold hands. What was it with these two? Did they know each other? They looked close. In fact he had to admit they looked good together, *right* together. But the way they were talking earlier, he wasn't sure it had been a romantic liaison. It had looked more businesslike. Yet after the note had been exchanged – the note that had made Flanders turn pale – things had changed. Business had been done, and maybe things moved on to pleasure. Yes, that's what it was. The note was the business.

He'd followed them out of the steakhouse, crossed the road and cut into an alleyway. From the shadows he watched them continue their conversation and eventually hold hands. He had been surprised they hadn't kissed. But then when she turned from him there was something about her body language that suggested that the holding hands had been everything that she was prepared to give.

Once Flanders had turned away from the departing girl, Adams stepped out from the alleyway and started walking fast, closing in on her with every step.

CHAPTER EIGHT

The moon wasn't full, but it was close, and it looked pure large and silver in the Texas sky. There was something sh read once, a poem in which two lovers looked at the mo from many miles apart at the same time and in doing so felt or maintained – a connection.

As she turned into East Cedar Street, Rosalie Robertson wondered if the intriguing Jim Jackson might be looking at the moon right now. Was he thinking of her? Did he feel what she felt? Was it right that they – assuming he felt it, too – should or could feel this way after just a day or two?

Then she told herself she was being nonsensical. He was probably thinking about his friend Leon and what they were going to do together once Jim had rescued him. And what if Jim got caught? Wasn't that the most likely outcome? How could one man rescue another from a prison?

No, whichever way you looked at it, he was gone and wouldn't be coming back, no matter how romantic the moon and stars made one feel.

She gazed at the moon for a moment longer, not wanting to give up the fantasy, and in that moment someone grabbed her wrist so tightly that pain lanced up her arm. She opened her mouth to scream and felt the barrel of a gun jabbed hard into her spine.

'It's cocked and my finger is on the trigger,' a man said, his

'Note?'

He closed his eyes briefly. He sighed, then opened his hands in front of him and looked at them as if puzzled at what he saw.

'It's been a long day. I've walked more miles than you know. I've stood in the hot sun longer that I should have. I'm tired. What was in the note?'

Now she realized what he meant. The note she had handed to Jim.

'You were watching us. You were spying on us.'

He interlocked his fingers and turned his hands round so that the palms of his hands face outwards and he stretched his arms and his fingers cracked.

'I meant it when I said I'm the good guy. My job is to protect the likes of you. Well, not just you. Maybe not you at all. Maybe everyone else. It depends on how we get along over the next few minutes.'

She shivered. The shivers became a shudder. Her insides churned.

'What did the note say?'

No, she was not going to tell him. He was not a good guy. A good guy did not force a young woman off the street at gunpoint. A good guy did not bring that young woman into a deserted storeroom with bloodstains on the floor.

She shook her head.

'What does that mean? You don't know? You don't want to tell me?'

She wished he would speak louder. The quietness of his voice, almost a whisper, was unnerving.

Once, in Kansas, she had seen the body of a man hanging from a tree. There had been thousands of flies crawling over the corpse and the eyes were missing. 'A rustler,' a local farmer had said, 'We left him there as a warning to the rest of the gang.' The farmer's voice had been quiet, too. Quiet and harsh, almost a rasp. When Rosalie had looked closer she had noticed a long scar across the man's throat. He saw her looking and said, 'That was a card-cheat. I called him out and sure enough he had the Jack of Hearts in his pocket. He cut my throat on the way out the door but the doc stitched me up.' The farmer had smiled. 'A fellow walking by tripped him up. I mean he tripped up the cheater, not the doctor. We hanged him, too. I mean the cheater, not the fellow who tripped him up.' Then the farmer had winked. That's how it had been out there in the west. There was scary stuff but it had always already happened, or was about to happen.

Here, the bad stuff was actually happening.

'Who are you?' she asked, trying to buy time. Her hands were shaking. She wiped her nose. She swallowed and tensed her stomach, trying to maintain some sense of calm. She had survived a country where they hanged rustlers and let the birds eat their eyes; she could survive this.

'I ask the questions.'

She could tell him that she didn't know what was in the note. But then he'd want to know who wrote it and that would implicate Roberta. She could tell him what it said – but that would be like giving up Jim. It was unthinkable.

She could make something up. Yes, that was the thing to do. But what?

Think!

'Last chance,' he said. 'What was in that note you gave to. . . .' He paused. 'You tell me his name, too.'

He doesn't know Jim's name, she thought. Her mind was whirling. It was too hard to think. She was suddenly very hot as if a great fire had been set right in front of her. Sweat rolled down the sides of her face and down her back and sides.

'Give me your hand,' the man said.

'What?'

He stepped forward and, despite not being that tall, it felt like he towered above her. His shape blocked out the minimal light. He took her right hand. She tried to pull it away but he held it firm.

'I hate to hurt a pretty woman,' he said. 'But. . . .'

Then he bent a finger back so far and so fast that it snapped like a dry twig. Pain exploded within her hand, her arm, and her shoulder. It was as if a stick of dynamite had lit up a silent darkness with the loudest roar and the brightest light imaginable. She screamed and he clamped his hand over her mouth. She writhed like a snake that someone had driven a pitchfork through. She sobbed through his foul-tasting fingers, and he held her tight: her face, her hand, her whole body.

When he let her go she jumped from the chair and ran to a corner of the room, pressing her hand against her breast. The tears came and it was hard to breathe in between the violent sobs. Her legs trembled and then gave way and she found herself on the floor, the oil lamp flickering and in the dancing pools of light she saw the blood stains once again.

'Now,' the man said, still very quietly, 'are you ready to answer my questions?'

It was midnight.

The streets were quiet, just a few people stumbling around where the taverns and hotels remained open.

Jim Jackson moved through the shadows, his saddle-bags, which contained a few clothes, a few books and all else he owned, over his shoulders. It was a good time to leave town – in the dark, with people moving towards sleep rather than wakefulness.

He had found what he had come to find – and thinking now of Rosalie he wondered if he hadn't found something more, too. But he pushed such thoughts from his mind. They were thoughts for another time. For now his attention had to be on his old friend Leon. He had to find Leon and figure a way of getting him away from wherever he was.

And then?

Then there was a story to share with Leon. A story of a man

called Anderson in a place called Leyton, Texas.

Jim Jackson rested his hand on the gun at his hip. Sam McRae's gun. McRae, who had arrested Jim all those years ago. Just a few months back, in Parker's Crossing, New Mexico, Sam McRae had located Jim Jackson and had apologised for that arrest. Or rather, not for the arrest, but for the subsequent conviction for a murder that McRae had come to know Jim Jackson hadn't committed. McRae had been killed in that New Mexico town and Jackson had exacted a suitable revenge. But before he had died, McRae had told him about Anderson.

'Over in Leyton, Texas, there's a fellow named Jack Anderson who's been talking up a killing he did during a train robbery some twelve years ago,' McRae had said. 'Are you listening to me, Jim?'

'Yep. Fellow I never heard of called Anderson killed someone in a place I never heard of.'

'He didn't kill anyone in Leyton. That's where he lives now. He's a tough guy and he's trying hard to build a tougher reputation. He's talking about killing a Texas Ranger during a train robbery.'

Jim knew that he hadn't killed a Texas Ranger in their final ever train robbery. And he knew that Leon hadn't either. Leon had been up on the footplate taking care of the driver and fireman.

But someone had.

They'd all worn black hats and black bandanas. Black coats, too. Hans Freidlich, the leader, had once said, 'Perhaps they'll call us the Black Mask gang?' The idea had been that they all looked alike, that after each robbery there's be no way of identifying individuals.

Of course, it hadn't really happened like that. Even masked and hatted, Jim Jackson had developed a reputation as the gentleman. He'd always been polite and kind to the women; he often let them keep engagement or wedding rings. At his trial that girl had even testified that the gentleman hadn't been the killer.

Such testimony had stood for nothing.

Someone had wanted him convicted for murder and so it had been.

Leon, too.

And they had strung up Hans, shot poor Billy Moore, and Patrick had died in Huntsville.

They'd all been set up and McRae had suggested it was by a fellow called Anderson in Leyton, Texas.

Well, he and Leon would be paying that fellow a visit.

He could see the livery up ahead. It was dark save for one window behind which a soft light flickered. Yes, this was a good time for leaving Austin. That damn train robbery on the way in could have spoiled everything. He'd wanted to come in and leave quietly. Well he'd come in shooting. But at least he managed to keep his head down ever since, and luckily for him no one had found out who he really was.

'His name is Jim Jackson,' Adams said.

Maxwell Higgs wasn't happy. He was in a dressing gown although he hadn't yet retired upstairs when Adam's had started knocking on his door.

'You've come here at midnight to tell me you've found out the fellow's name?'

'No. I've come here to tell you that he was a train robber—'

'He *foiled* a train robbery just yesterday.'

'Exactly. He knows how they work. He's not scared by masked fellows shouting. He knows how to handle a gun.'

'Like lightning.'

'Exactly.'

'It still could have waited until morning.'

But the truth was Maxwell Higgs was excited. These were good times for the Houston and Texas Central Railroad. They had two men dead over at the mortuary – and the interest from the townsfolk had been incredible. Folks had been coming in and out all day. Some several times. It was only because of the concern over the growing smell of the bodies that he had decided not to hold a second day's viewing. Then there were those two fellows over in the jailhouse. One had a broken arm and the other a sore head. They'd both soon have broken necks. There'd been a growing concern over train robberies and the board were concerned it would shortly start to impact business. But Higgs was leading the way in beating the robbers. He could see a promotion on the horizon. And most definitely a pay-rise.

'Sherry?' he said, walking over to his sideboard. He lifted a decanter.

'Sure. Thank you.'

'So Daniel Flanders was a made-up name. I told you.'

'Yep.'

'I assume there's more?'

'Oh, yes.'

Higgs handed Adams a sherry glass. 'Good health.' They clinked glasses. 'It sounds like you've been busy. Tell me the rest.'

'He did ten years, this Jim Jackson.'

'Where?'

'Right here in Texas.'

'And he's come back. Brave or foolish.'

'He was part of a gang and they're all dead. Except one.'

'Go on.'

'Leon Winters. Leasing Camp 13. Prairie City, Madison County. That's exactly how she said it.'

'Who's *she*?'

'The young lady who told me all of this.'

Higgs sipped his sherry. 'I trust you were nice to her. I don't want any more complaints.'

'We came to an understanding rather quickly.'

'So he's a train robber who did time in Texas and an old colleague is still alive. Why did he come back?'

'To find out where his colleague was. The records are here in Austin.'

'Ah. Now I understand. So the assumption is that he's about to try and do something about this Leon Winters?'

'Indeed it is.'

'Where is he staying?'

'The Alamo.'

'And I offered him the Washington.'

'He's a train robber. The Alamo is much more his style.'

'So let me get this straight. He did his time but now we believe he's going to head up to . . . don't tell me . . .' Higgs prided himself on his memory. 'Camp 13, Madison County.'

'Prairie City.'

'Yes. Do we know who's in charge up there?'

'No. But I'll wire them first thing in the morning.'

'And you'll follow him?'

'Yes. I had a fellow up at the livery with instructions not to let Jackson leave. But now I've told him to stand down. We know where Jackson's going. And we know he's going tomorrow.'

'And the moment he tries something. . . .'

'We'll be waiting.'

CHAPTER NINE

Red Kelly said, 'Who has visitors at midnight?'

Callum Short said, 'I visited a few places at midnight in my time. Cathouses, mostly.'

'And you were always out by five past,' Ned Donovan said.

'Boys, shut up,' Red said.

They were across the street from Maxwell Higgs' impressive house. It stood alone in a well-kept plot of land, looking very white and clean in the moonlight.

It had been easy enough to find out where Higgs lived. They'd just waited at the station – well, they'd waited in the saloon across from the station, nursing beers for as long as they could, watching Ned squirm, trying to find a comfortable position to sit. A fellow had been playing a piano and a poker game had been in progress, but the three of them had kept themselves to themselves, drinking and watching the clock behind the bar tick round. They took turns standing outside waiting for Higgs. Around five o'clock Ned saw the man walking out with a leather satchel in his hand. They'd followed him all the way home. Simple.

'We'll do it late,' Red said. 'When he's gone to bed. He'll be most vulnerable then.'

They'd waited hours for Maxwell Higgs' lights to all go off, but then, when there was just one light left burning and they were debating as to whether or not they ought to make their move, a fellow had walked up the street, opened the gate on Higgs' little fence and rapped on his door. The boys had shifted backwards into the shadows of the tree-filled yard across the street, and had waited some more.

The man was in there fifteen or twenty minutes, and it wasn't long after he left that the last light went off.

'Five minutes,' Red said. It had been a day of waiting. They could manage five more minutes.

'Who was that?' Marion Higgs said. 'I hope you told them how rude it is to be calling at such an hour.'

She was in bed. A candle burned on the small table beside the bed. She had two pillows propping her not inconsiderable body into a comfortable position, and she had a book resting face down on her chest.

'It was Ben Adams.'

'That brute. He wouldn't care whether he was the rudest man in the world or not.'

'He's not a brute and he's not rude. In fact he's a quiet—'

'I know he's *quiet*. But from what I hear he's the cruellest man in Austin.'

'He does what he needs to do.'

'And what needed to be done in our house at midnight?'

Maxwell Higgs took off his dressing gown and hung it on the back of the door.

'He had some news he wanted to share.'

'And it couldn't wait until morning?'

'He might be gone first thing in the morning. Tracking a man.'

'Tracking a man? Now that does sound like something Ben Adams would get up early for. Who is this man?'

'A fellow named Jim Jackson. A train robber. He's come to Texas to try and break out some of his old gang from prison.' He pulled the covers back on his side of the bed and climbed in. 'With a bit of luck we'll catch him in the act and—'

'*We'll* catch him? Are you going too?'

'I'm speaking figuratively. *We* being the Railroad.'

'Oh. That *we*. Anyway, darling, before you get too comfortable, you wouldn't get me a glass of water, would you?'

'Of course, darling.'

Maxwell Higgs climbed out of bed and went downstairs.

'Don't move,' Red Kelly said, pressing the barrel of his gun against the back of Maxwell Higgs' neck.

Higgs froze. One hand was on a jug of water he kept on the counter, and the other was holding the cloth they kept over the top of the jug to stop any spiders getting in there.

'Put your hands in the air slowly,' Red said.

'Who are you?' Higgs said, raising his hands.

'That don't matter.'

'What do you want?'

'Don't turn around.'

'I won't.'

'Those boys you had on display today.'

'It wasn't a display. It was—'

'You had 'em on display.'

'OK. OK.'

'You said one of your guards shot 'em.'

'You're the feller was talking to me—'

'I said don't turn.'

'OK.'

'What's the guard's name?'

'I'm sorry. As I told you earlier, I'm not at—' Higgs let out a hiss of pain as Red twisted the gun barrel into his neck.

'Name. And where I can find him.'

'I'm sorry—' Red twisted the barrel again and this time Higgs' pain was louder, a cry rather than a hiss.

'Are you OK, Maxwell?' a woman called from above. 'It wasn't another spider in the water was it?'

Red Kelly looked around at Callum Short. 'Seems like we

have the fellow's wife upstairs. Go on up and say hello.'

'Wait,' Higgs said. 'Please. I can't tell you the fellow's name.'

'Upstairs,' Red said, nodding to Callum.

'I don't know the man,' Higgs said.

'That's not what you told me earlier.'

'Our guards. I don't know every one of them. I swear.'

Upstairs, Marion Higgs exclaimed, 'Who are you? How dare you—' Then her voice cut off abruptly.

'What is he doing?' Higgs said.

'Don't worry about that,' Red said, still talking to the back of Higgs' head. 'You were about to tell me the man's name.'

'I don't know—'

'Fellow shoots two men on your railroad and you don't know his name?'

'Flanders. Daniel Flanders. That was his name.'

'So you did know his name.'

'Yes, yes. Please. I've told you his name now—'

'Where can I find Daniel Flanders?'

'I don't know. Really. *Honestly.*'

'Let's go upstairs,' Red Kelly said. 'I'd like to meet your wife.'

'Please, I don't know where he is.'

'Upstairs. And if you try anything I'll shoot you in the spine. You'll never walk again.'

Higgs turned and, with his hands in the air and his night-shirt billowing about his legs, he led Red Kelly upstairs.

In the bedroom Callum Short had his revolver pointed at Marion Higgs. He had a finger over his lips indicating her to be quiet. She was still propped up in bed, her mouth open and her skin pale yellow in the flickering candlelight.

When her husband shuffled into the room at gunpoint her mouth opened wider and then, his presence giving her the courage to find her voice, she said, 'Maxwell, who are these men?' She looked at Red. 'Who are you?'

'Your husband couldn't remember a fellow's name,' Red said. 'Then he did. Right now he can't remember where I can find that fellow, but he's about to.'

'I honestly don't know,' Higgs said.

'Cal',' Red said. 'Grab that pillow.' He nodded towards the pillow on the empty side of the bed.

'What are you going to do?' Higgs said.

'I'm probably going to shoot you in the back,' Red said, 'and leave you squirming on the floor in agony, praying that you bleed out quickly because of the pain. That's if you try anything. On the other hand, if you tell me what I need to know then I'll just go.'

Callum slipped his gun back into his holster, walked around the bed, and picked up the pillow. Marion Higgs pulled the blanket up to her throat.

'What are you doing?' she said. She looked at Higgs. 'Do something.'

'Over her face,' Red said.

'No!' Higgs said.

Callum was quick. He jumped on to the bed and, before Marion could move, he had the pillow pressed over her face. He climbed on top of her, using his own weight to hold her down as she thrashed and squirmed. One of her flailing arms caught Callum a heavy blow on the side of the head and knocked his hat off, but he kept pressing the pillow down.

'No!' Higgs said and jumped forwards. Red had hold of Higgs' nightshirt collar but the shirt ripped and came loose in Red's hand. A naked Maxwell Higgs launched himself at Callum Short, knocking him off the bed. Callum crashed into the bedside cabinet. The burning candle arced through the air and came to rest against the wall. On the bed Marion Higgs was gasping for breath and weeping.

Higgs, on his knees on top of Marion – just like Callum had been a moment earlier – turned and looked at Red.

'You sonofabitch,' he said.

With the knocking over of the candle the shadows in the room had changed. Higgs' face was in darkness. He turned to Marion and said, 'Are you all right?'

She sobbed and tried to breathe. She coughed.

'Easy,' Higgs said.

On the far side of the bed Callum Short stood up. He still had the pillow in his hand. The candle was burning behind him, up against the wall. From where Red was standing Callum was just a silhouette. It was like watching a creature rise up out of the darkness, made more terrifying because you couldn't see any details.

'You shouldn't have done that, old man,' Callum said.

'Get away!' Higgs said, turning his gaze from Red to Callum.

Red ratcheted back the hammer on his Colt.

'Time for me to shoot someone, I think. Maybe both of you. But who wants to go first?'

'Tell . . . them,' Marion Higgs said, her voice quiet and hoarse and broken by her snatched gasps for air. 'Tell them what . . . they want to know. Tell them about . . . Jim Jackson.'

It was lighter in the room now, as if the candle flame had grown larger.

'Jim Jackson?' Red said.

Higgs rolled backwards on the bed. He snatched at one edge of the blanket, trying to pull it across his body to cover his nakedness.

'You told us the fellow's name was Daniel Flanders.'

'It is. It was.'

'You lied.'

'No.'

'Cal, the pillow again.'

'No!' Higgs said, trying to untangle himself from the blanket and holding out his arms to push Callum away from Marion.

Red stepped forwards and placed the cocked gun against

Higgs' head.

'Just tell us all about this Jim Jackson and we'll go.'

'I don't—'

'Max!' Marion said. The shadow of the pillow was over her face. 'The room is on fire!'

A quick glance was all Red needed. Yep, the candle had rolled up against the wall. The wallpaper had turned black and was now smoking. Actual flames were starting to curl upwards.

'The house is on fire,' Higgs said, looking at Red. 'Please!'

'Plenty of time to put it out,' Red said. 'I mean, you have a jug of water downstairs.'

'Maxwell!' Marion pleaded. 'Tell them!'

'The pillow, Cal.'

'Tell them!'

Outside, Ned Donovan, keeping guard with instructions to shoot into the night sky as a warning should Red and Callum need to get out straight away, thought he heard a gunshot from inside the house. He had one hand down the back of his breeches and was trying to work a piece of lead loose from the top of his thigh. The wound had scabbed over, but the metal was still in his leg and bothered him every time he touched it or sat on it. He had picked the scab off and was busy trying to squeeze the metal out. It hurt like hell and he knew he had another dozen or more other pieces in his flesh, some that he couldn't reach very well, but he was darned if he was going to ask Red or Cal to do it. The noise from the house had been quiet and muffled and he'd been breathing noisily through clenched teeth when he had heard it. After brief consideration he decided it had probably been a window slamming.

A moment later he heard another. This one, because he was paying more attention, was most definitely a gunshot.

He stared at the house, wondering what was going on in there, and now he saw tendrils of smoke rising from one side, up on the first floor.

He pulled his hand out of his trousers and drew his gun, holding it down by his side.

The smoke was thickening.

Red and Callum suddenly appeared along the side of the house, running. They nodded towards Ned to follow them, and then they were gone, into the darkness along the street.

Ned ran after them, pausing only once to look back, and when he did he saw flames licking at the wall that a few moments previously had only been smoking.

That was the thing about Red, he thought. If the fellow wanted something he would do anything.

Anything.

CHAPTER TEN

Billy Burke, the young prison guard, found Webster T. Ellington by the gate. It seemed to Billy that Webster spent a lot of time by that gate, almost as if it was him rather than the prisoners that was imprisoned by it.

'Captain wants to see you,' Billy said.

Webster spat tobacco juice on the ground. Billy knew that it riled Webster whenever someone used the word "captain" and it wasn't him they were talking about. Webster had been a captain once. Still was as far as he was concerned. But the thing was, they had a *real* captain, too. And you had to call him by his proper title, no matter that it riled Webster.

'What about?'

'Said there's news from Austin that would interest you.'

Webster glared at Billy.

'Last time, and the time before, and the time before that, the news from Austin was that I was being moved from one camp to another. Usually somewhere hotter, or wetter, or colder. Or somewhere that stank more. I doubt this time will be any different.'

'You never know.'

'It's been nice knowing you, kid.'

Billy watched Webster stomp off towards the house. That was where the captain lived and where he had his office. Webster's shoulders were hunched over as if he had the weight of the world upon them.

Billy looked across at the huts. It was eight-thirty in the morning. The prisoners were already two hours into their working day over in the forest, felling and cutting and digging and hauling. Most of the guards were down there with them. Billy had the job of keeping an eye on the half dozen men who were too sick to work. They were in the hut over there by the foul-smelling creek. One of them would be allowed out to empty buckets and get water, but the rule was, if you were too ill to work then you were too ill to walk around the compound.

The one named Winters was in there.

Winters only came to mind because Webster had a special hatred for the fellow. Webster told how Winters reminded him of another fellow. Billy had forgotten the other fellow's name, but he was the cause of all Webster's issues. And Webster often took out those issues on Winters, which was probably why he was lying up in his bunk right now, baking in the heat and counting down the minutes until water time.

Billy looked back towards the house. It was a massive brick-built mansion that could have been accommodated all the guards' living quarters, not just the captain and his family. Little Alfie – the captain's son – was around somewhere. He was just six years old. The kid always had a big smile on his face and his hair stuck up all over the place. He loved to help out and do odd jobs around the camp, running this way and that, usually with his little dog close behind him. They let Alfie open and close the gates sometime when visitors arrived, and they let him replace the paper stack in the privy once all the prisoners had gone off to the lumber camp.

Billy saw Webster now, coming back from seeing the captain, walking past the long bunkhouse where the guards lived. He was smiling and his shoulders no longer looked so hunched over.

'Good news?' Billy said when Webster had got back to the gate.

'Oh yes,' Webster said nodding. 'An old friend is coming to visit.'

'An old friend?'

'Uh-huh.'

'You're pleased, I can tell. Is he a good friend?'

Webster smiled.

CHAPTER ELEVEN

Prairie City was, Jim Jackson thought, anything but a city. It was a town, at best, and a small one at that. Whoever had named it must have been hoping for greater things. It had a main street lined by false-fronted buildings with facades that had either never been painted or that had faded in the Texas sun. The boardwalk was broken in places and the thoroughfare was carved with wagon ruts. Clouds of dust swirled at ankle level. Main Street was criss-crossed with smaller streets, each lined with more plain timber businesses. Further out, there was no pattern to the buildings. They had seemingly been erected at random points wherever the ground was flat enough and solid enough to support them. A few miles to the west and north the green hills were thick with lumber, and from those hills a creek ran down to the eastern side of Prairie City. Someone had run clay pipes from the creek to the centre of town where it looked like a small pumping handle would draw water. But when Jim led his horse to a trough alongside the pumping handle he saw that the trough was dry. It was a few hundred yards to the creek. Maybe it was too much effort to pump that water. Prairie Creek had the air of a town where an awful lot of things were too much trouble.

He followed the dry pipes over to the creek and watered his horse, and when she'd had her fill they came back into town. He looped the reins over the hitching rail outside an unnamed saloon and walked inside.

He ordered a beer and the bartender poured it from a cask that sat on a chair behind the counter. The beer was warm and cloudy but it washed the dust from Jim's throat.

'You have rooms here?' he asked.

The bartender was tall and thin and had a bald head. He wore a white shirt and a blue vest. The shirt was dirty at the collar and cuffs.

'Not here. There's a hotel a little further along. I'm sure they'll fit you in.'

'Thanks.'

'No idea how they make that place pay,' the bartender said. He shrugged and pulled a puzzled expression as if the economies of his fellow businessmen were one of the great mysteries of life.

'Not the sort of place that sees many visitors?'

'Nothing here but lumber,' the bartender said.

'Uh-huh. Lumber.'

'You don't look like a lumber man.'

'I'm visiting a friend up at Camp 13.'

'Camp 13, huh?' The bartender shook his head.

'You know it?'

'I've heard of it. I've heard *about* it.'

The man's expression suggested that Camp 13 was just about the worst place on God's own earth.

'Not good?'

'If your friend works there it might be OK. If he's a prisoner, then . . .' The bartender shook his head. 'I've heard it's a pretty cruel place.'

'Can you point me in the right direction?'

'Sure. Follow the creek north. After about an hour's ride the creek splits. Follow the right-hand water. There's a trail there. It goes uphill – well, the water's coming down – and it splits again. Keep following the right-hand trail and there's Camp 13.'

'Much obliged.'

'My pleasure. Another beer?'

Between the saloon and the hotel was a hardware shop. In the window display were spades and picks and hammers, a bag of nails, a set of spurs artfully positioned on a box of shotgun shells, several leather belts hanging from a bent wire, two hats, a water canteen and, stretched out to its full length, a four-section telescope made from brass and mahogany.

Jim paused. Money wasn't an issue, but he did have to be careful. He wasn't making any at the moment and he did seem to be spending it rather quickly. He'd given a fortune away back in Parker's Crossing, New Mexico. Blood money. They were buying a bell for the church. Most folks couldn't understand why he'd given it all away. But the money – proceeds from all those train robberies – had brought nothing but pain and death. He was better rid of it. All he'd kept was enough to see him through what he needed to do.

The telescope was a dollar. He haggled and got it for seventy-five cents.

He booked a room at the hotel and then bedded his horse down at the livery.

Tomorrow he'd follow the creek up into the hills.

The next day, late morning, he rode the trail into the hills. It felt good to be far away from Austin. He hadn't realized how oppressive the city had been – all those buildings, all those people. It was strange; such things had been his life once. He'd always assumed that one day he'd return to city life but something had changed. Nowadays, he preferred the freedom of the open spaces. He liked the solitude, too – albeit even as the thought crossed his mind he found himself thinking of Rosalie. There was solitude and there was loneliness. He enjoyed the first and didn't suffer from the second. But there was *something* – just a small space that was no longer filled.

That was another thing: for years, for all that time when he was imprisoned and suffering, for those long nights when he tried desperately to keep thoughts and memories locked up because it hurt too much otherwise, it was always Jennifer whom he thought of when he weakened. Jennifer, back in Illinois, with the wide streets and tall buildings and bright lights. Jennifer, for whom he had ventured west. Yet now it was Rosalie he was thinking of. Rosalie and the open spaces and freedom.

He left his horse in the tree line and, crouching low, worked his way forward to the long dark grass on the edge of a deforested slope. He looked down upon Prison Leasing Camp 13.

A high fence encircled the camp. A creek flowed beneath the fence and ran within spitting distance of a series of wooden huts. Behind the huts there was a smaller hut constructed on a platform overhanging the creek. The privy, Jim guessed. In front of the huts was an open area. There were water troughs and there was a pole. Jim shivered when he saw the pole. It was a whipping pole. The yard had no shelter. Even if they weren't planning on whipping a feller they could simply tie him up and let the sun roast him. There was a gate in the fence and beyond the gate a track led up to a large brick house. Hell, it was bigger than large. It was a mansion. It would have fitted right on to Capitol Avenue back in Austin. Outside the fence there were a couple of guard posts. They were raised up but not very high, and they were empty. On the far side of the camp, maybe a half a mile outside the wire, there were stacks and stacks of lumber, piled neatly. A wide track led from the lumber yard up into the hills, and another stretched southwards out of sight behind a low rise.

Jim turned the telescope back on the camp. It looked deserted. He scanned it inch by inch. A movement caught his eye. Someone was coming out of one of the privies, hitching up his trousers, a rifle lodged between his arm and his torso as he wrestled with his belt. A young man. A guard. Jim watched the man walk towards the far hut and open the door. He said something to someone inside, closed the door, and walked over to the gate. He opened the gate, walked through, and took up station on the other side.

A few minutes later an old man emerged from the hut. He was hunched over and walked with a cane. In his free hand he carried a jug. The man shuffled over to one of the washing troughs, filled the jug up with water, and then turned and retraced his steps. As he turned the man looked up at the sky and Jim caught his face full on in the telescope. The man wasn't old after all. Probably wasn't even as old as Jim. But he was so thin his face looked like nothing but skin stretched over bones. His eyes were dark holes. His shirt was soiled and torn and it hung on his thin shoulders like a wretched flag blown by the wind and caught on autumn tree branches. The man edged back towards the hut, spilling much of the water he had taken so long to fetch. Jim watched until he went back inside the hut. As the door opened Jim caught sight of another man inside.

The sick hut.

That's why there was only one guard. If you were sick enough not to be working you would be in no fit state to make a run for freedom.

He continued to scan the camp. There were no hound dogs. That was good. He didn't have a plan yet, but not having bloodhounds on your trail would be a positive thing. A couple of times he saw a young boy, couldn't have been no more than six, run down to the gate and talk to the guard. The kid was smiling. And actually there was a dog, a little terrier of some sort that was close to that kid's heels almost all of the time. But it was no bloodhound. At one point the kid ran down to the privy with a handful of paper squares. When he came out he ran over to the gate and held his nose and pulled a face. The guard laughed. The kid ran off to the big house.

Jim crawled back to his horse, drank water and ate some beef jerky he'd bought in town. He circled the camp and looked at the place from as many different angles as he could. Mid-afternoon, things became interesting briefly when a group of three riders arrived at the camp, talked to the young guard, then headed off to the mansion house. They didn't stay long and they didn't look like guards or lawmen.

Just before dusk, over on the far hillside, Jim Jackson noticed a dust cloud rising up. It was created by the feet of a couple of dozen prisoners and guards on horses. Jim Jackson lay in the long grass and watched as the gang came closer. He scanned their faces, one by one, looking for his old friend.

Leon wasn't there.

He checked every face a second time.

A feeling of disappointment rose inside him. Had he been given poor information?

He checked a third time and still he couldn't find Leon.

He watched the prisoners being counted in through the gate. Once inside the first thing they all did was to walk over and cup their hands in the warm trough water and drink and pour it over their dusty heads. One wandered over to the sick hut, opened the door and said something. And, just for a second, there was Leon Winters. His old buddy came to the door and handed out the same jug that Jim had watched the other sick man fill up earlier. Leon, as tall as ever and still standing straight but now as thin as the whipping pole in the yard and as pale as the dust that caked the prisoners. Then Leon was gone, back inside the sick hut.

But he was there.

And he was alive.

Jim put down the telescope and balled his fists in delight.

He looked down at the camp again; the shadows were long now and he saw a different guard walking over towards the gate. There was something about the way the guard walked, about the way he moved.

The hairs on Jim's neck bristled.

He raised the telescope. He focused on the new guard.

A fear wrapped itself around his spine as real as if a field surgeon with ice-cold hands had opened his flesh and taken hold of his bones. He actually felt his bowels and bladder weaken and had to clench his muscles to control himself. Memories came flooding back so fast and strong, so hard and real, that his hands began shaking and he dropped the glass. He realized once more why he'd spent so long drunk when he'd finally been released from his own prison camp. It had been to forget about Captain Ellington, a man whom, for years, Jim Jackson had considered the Devil on Earth. The man who had caused him more suffering than any other. A man who had told him that if he ever set foot in Texas again, what had come before would be nothing compared to what would come next.

That man was down there guarding Leon.

CHAPTER TWELVE

Ben Adams, alongside George Dubois and Whittaker Gordon – another of Adams' Houston and Texas Central Railroad guards – sat at a window table in the Prairie Creek Saloon. It was dark outside, but moonlight shone through the window. An oil lamp burned on their table, as one did on every table. More lights were suspended from the ceiling. The room smelled of fire and sweat, of beer and whiskey.

'Do we need to go back to Austin?' Dubois said. He was young, lean and full of energy. Like a dog that had been given a scent to follow he was itching to follow the trail, itching to catch this fellow, Jim Jackson, who had brought them to Prairie City.

'Keep your voice down,' Adams said quietly.

'He never heard nothing,' Gordon said. 'He's too drunk.'

Over at the bar the man they had come for was drinking beer and whiskey as if the entire Texas supply was liable to run out soon.

'It doesn't do any harm to keep things to ourselves,' Adams said.

'So?' Dubois whispered.

A couple of hours earlier they'd ridden up to the camp to introduce themselves to the captain and discovered a message waiting for them. Maxwell Higgs was dead. His wife, too. There'd been a fire at their house back in Austin.

'Charlie Entwhistle has got things covered, I'm sure. We do what we came to do. We wait until he—' Adams nodded towards the man drinking at the bar '—makes his move. Then we catch him in the act.'

Adams didn't know if the fire at Higgs' house was related. He didn't think so. How could it be? It was most probably a terrible coincidence. It was a shame, too. He'd liked Higgs and they'd had a good working relationship. Still, when they took Jim Jackson back, one-time train robber and now about to break another train robber out of prison, whoever was in charge would have to be impressed.

'Perhaps we could have a drink?' Whit said. 'He sure ain't going to be making his move this evening.' Whit was just a kid, like Dubois. They were both restless and full of energy.

Adams was about to say that they were on duty, that it always paid to keep a clear head. But he paused. He'd driven the boys hard on the ride up here and they'd been out riding all day. And Whit was right. This Jim Jackson fellow was going to be good for nothing for a long time.

'Yeah, why not? Just keep away from this place in case you start talking too loud again.' He smiled. 'You boys head across the street and have your fill.'

'You're a good man, boss,' George Dubois said.

He knew he had to stop. He could feel himself sliding back down into darkness that not so long ago he had thought he would never escape. That he had escaped, that he had somehow crawled back up into the daylight, was a miracle that he didn't think he could manage twice. Yet he couldn't stop. Seeing the captain in close up through the glass had brought it all back to him in one massive hit. It was like the man had appeared, not hundreds of yards away, but actually inside his head. Jim didn't recall much of the ride back to town, only that he was shaking as if it was winter and they had stripped him naked and tied him to a whipping post – which *had* happened. It had been the captain that had instigated it.

Back in Prairie City with his horse stabled, he recalled ordering that first beer and that first whiskey, and then a second. When those drinks hadn't stopped the shaking he had ordered more – just like the old days – and had kept going until now, whenever now was, and he could at last feel his heart slowing down, and his nerves settling. But he'd drank so much he'd had to sit down on a bar stool instead if standing, and that fellow behind the counter with no hair and the dirty white shirt was giving him a look as if to say *I don't want any trouble.* Jim figured he'd reassure the bartender but forming the words seemed too much trouble, so he simply pushed the glass forward for one more drink.

Across the street, in the Echo Valley Bar, Red Kelly asked the bartender if there was anyone new in town.

'Funnily enough, those two fellows there are new.'

'Those two young fellows? Both of them?'

'Yep,' the bartender said. 'Never seen either of them before.'

'I was expecting just one fellow.'

The barman shrugged. 'It's not a big town. But we ain't the only bar. You'd be better off asking at the hotel. There's only one hotel.'

Red nodded. 'Yeah, that's not a bad idea.'

He took three drinks back to the table where Ned Donovan and Callum Short were sitting.

'Any luck?' Ned said. He fidgeted on the hard seat. The ride up here hadn't done the wounds in his legs and buttocks any favours.

'Those two fellows talking to the girls are both new in town.'

'Thought this Jim Jackson was riding alone?' Callum said.

'Red, I thought you'd seen him," Ned said. 'On the train.'

'Yes and no. I didn't see his face. There was a boy with wide shoulders in the way. Jackson was tall, though. I know that much. Taller than either of those fellers over there.'

'So what's the plan?' Callum said.

'In the morning we'll watch the hotel,' Red said. 'Or maybe I'll just sweet-talk the clerk.'

'And when you find Jackson?'

'I'll kill him,' Red said. 'Once I've told him why I'm killing him.'

He woke up unsure of where he was. Pale curtains hung over a small window. He could see the shape of the moon through the thin material. His head hurt. It felt as if someone had let loose an unbroken stallion in there. He felt nauseous. His insides twisted and turned and gurgled. He was still dressed, lying on the bed fully clothed, even his gun belt on.

He began to remember. A shiver of fear tried to form inside and he gritted his teeth and through force of will refused to let the fear harden and take shape. It would be easy to walk away, the easiest thing in the world. The most sensible thing, too. Maybe he should. Maybe what he was planning – no matter how vaguely – was just too ambitious, too unlikely, and too stupid. Why not simply head over to the livery, saddle up, and leave? He could be back across the border in a day or two. Never to step foot in Texas again. Never to risk his own skin and sanity again. Never to feel so much pain again. It would be easy. It would be sensible.

He sat up. The room rolled one way and then the other. The nausea rose inside him like a wave. But like a wave it settled.

He stood up, and again had to wait for the room to stop spinning.

There was a jug of water and a tin cup on a small table in the corner. He didn't feel like drinking water but he did anyway. Three cups was all he could manage and then, for a long time, it felt like the sickness wasn't going to settle. When it did, he drank a fourth cup of water. He felt sick again and prudence took him outside where the cool night air dried the sweat on his face.

Prairie City was silent. The sky was cloudless and a million stars sparkled. He found himself wondering if Rosalie was looking at those same stars. No, she'd be tucked up asleep in her sister's neat little Austin house and tomorrow she'd be going to work at her new job making up lists of people or whatever it was she did. He felt a sense of loss inside and this time his guts refused to settle and he vomited in the alleyway behind the hotel, bringing up water and not much else, but feeling better afterwards.

There was a faint glow in the sky over the eastern hills. It was pointless to return to his room now.

He walked towards the livery.

The sooner he did this thing the better. He had the inklings of a plan. Actually, he had two plans. One was brazen and upfront and involved simply marching into the camp with a gun in his hand. The fact that Leon was in the sick hut made this plan a whole lot more feasible than it might have been. If the only guard was that one he'd been watching yesterday then the plan would probably work. The trouble was it might involve killing the guard and it would certainly involve him and Leon needing to race across country long and hard to escape the chase. He wasn't sure that Leon would be up to that. He also wasn't sure that he could kill the guard in cold blood. But it was there as a plan if his other idea didn't work. The other idea wasn't much better. In fact it wasn't much of anything at all.

He needed to watch and learn a bit more before deciding. He also had to scout out the land around the camp. One more day, maybe two, and then he'd just have to do it, whichever way that turned out to be.

Adams said, 'He's not come out yet.'

The three railroad men, Adams, Dubois and Gordon, were

standing on the plank-walk across from the hotel, drinking strong coffee from tin cups. A young fellow just along the street had a fire going and was brewing up the coffee and selling it to passers-by. 'They don't like me over at the café or at the hotel,' the coffee seller said. 'But a man's got to make a living. I'm going to start frying bread soon. Wouldn't be surprised if I don't get shot then.' The young man had laughed as if he didn't care, but there had been nervousness to his laughter.

The coffee was bitter, smoky, and good, but after they'd downed two cups, Adams said, 'He mightn't come out till lunchtime. You two stay here and one of you come and get me if anything happens.'

'Where you going, boss?'

'To get some sleep and some breakfast. I'm not sure in what order. Whilst you two were drinking and whoring last night, I stayed up watching our man drink himself into oblivion. He lasted a long time.'

'Unlike Whit, here,' George said.

'Just as long as you,' Whit said.

'That's not what she told me.'

'Boys, you had your fun. Now let's be serious. You call me when you see him.'

The ride this morning felt longer, hotter, and harder than the previous day. Jim knew this was because he had slid into the darkness last night and had filled his body with poison. It had felt good at the time. Or rather, it had stopped him feeling bad. But he hadn't gone through everything in New Mexico to slip backwards into that previous way of living. He rested his hand on McRae's gun at his hip. They hadn't killed McRae for nothing back in the Crossing either. No, last night had been a one-off. The shock of seeing the captain again had snapped him back in time. But it wouldn't happen again.

He stopped at the creek, drank as much as he could, and

filled his waterskin. He was still shaking. Not through fear, though he did recognise that fear was present, deep inside, like a small warm rock. The shaking was his body's reaction to all that whiskey. He was glad that none of his friends back in Parker's Crossing had seen him. He had lived like that for months until breaking free of that life. People had died – some at his hand – to make it happen.

Whatever happened here, he wasn't going back to that life.

The sky was clear blue and cloudless. A hawk circled lazily on thermals. There was freshness in the air – the scent of grass and pine trees – and a very slight breeze that lifted the whiskey sweat from his skin.

He circled Camp 13 and found the creek that flowed down through the camp far below. He stopped in the thick copse of trees from which the creek emerged. Down below he saw the usual guard at the gate, the kid and his dog running back and forth over by the big house. He watched the dog chase a rabbit into the trees behind the house. The creek had, in wet years, worn quite a deep channel into the clay ground. The channel, coloured with parallel lines of clay in different hues of red and brown, ran behind the huts and, although it wasn't perfect, Jim saw that a man could probably crawl all the way up from the camp and into this copse of trees without being seen. Well, he would be seen if someone was looking carefully. But if there was something better to look at in the opposite direction, say where those massive piles of lumber were, and say it happened during the day when almost all of the guards were out in the timber fields, then that fellow would likely make it. He could even get beneath the fence where the creek flowed under the wire. Probably wouldn't even get his head wet. And if there was a horse waiting for him in this here copse of trees and if there was somewhere for them to head towards and hide out in, some water and some food waiting, a fellow might just get clean away. It wasn't a prison after all. It was just a lumber camp with one fence and a whole lot of fear holding men inside.

Jim looked up at the sun and estimated it was almost midday. Down in the camp yard the whipping pole cast no shadow.

He turned and rode in the opposite direction. In a couple of hours a man on a horse could get a fair distance in any direction. Unless they had a good tracker down there – and Jim had seen no evidence of such – then there was a good chance that they wouldn't be found.

All he needed now was somewhere to hide out.

It was going to be a hot day's riding, but he'd find somewhere and tomorrow he'd let Leon know what was coming.

'Son of a bitch,' Adams said, whispering, yet his voice as hard as flint. 'Here he comes now.'

'He wasn't in town after all,' George said.

'We knew that. But how did he lose us?' Adams said.

By lunchtime, when Jim Jackson hadn't emerged from the hotel, Adams had despatched Whittaker Gordon to the livery to see if Jim Jackson's horse – the grey – was still there. It wasn't. So they knew that Jackson had somehow evaded them: the question was whether he had done it deliberately or not. The consensus had been not – Jackson had no way of knowing that they were in town so why would he purposely sneak around? 'He doesn't know any of us. He never met us in Austin.' Adams had pointed out.

'Pure luck. Pure chance,' Dubois said.

'I don't like a lucky man,' Adams said.

Now, seeing Jackson riding in, looking tired but happy, his blue jacket and brown hat caked in dust, he said, 'Whit, you ride up to the lumber camp. Tell the captain up there that you're staying with him until this thing is over. Don't give him any choice.'

'Yes, sir.'

'George, tomorrow you watch his horse, I'll take the hotel. When he makes his move we'll be there one way or another.'

*

Jim had the boy at the livery give his horse a good rub down, and fresh food and water. She'd done well today. They'd covered a lot of miles and she hadn't complained once.

He walked back into the centre of Prairie City, pausing to buy a cup of coffee from a young lad who had set up an outside stall. He drank the coffee whilst leaning against a pole holding up a red awning outside the barber's shop and dentist. As far as he could tell the same fellow inside covered both professions. Across the street people wandered about, seemingly aimlessly, but there must have been a pattern to their existence, if only he could see it. Dogs, horses and people, all moving and stopping and standing and scratching. The air had the faint smell of horse manure and fire hanging in it.

He finished the coffee and gave the tin cup back to the vendor, and then he wandered over to the hardware store from where he'd bought his telescope two days before. This time he bought the large box of shotgun shells that the telescope had been resting on. He bought a cheap pen and a small bottle of ink. Across the street he bought a small rabbit from a butcher.

He went back to the hotel, pausing to pop into the outhouse round the back to steal some paper before heading up to his room.

Webster T. Ellington leaned against the gate and watched the sky darkening, the stars appearing one by one, the brightest first, then those that were smaller, fainter, and needing the darkness to fully form before they could be seen. He figured he was a little like those stars, the faint ones. He wasn't always noticed, wasn't always picked out as being the brightest or the best or the biggest. But by God when things got dark, when there was trouble around, he was a man who would be there.

He smiled. Yes, sir, things were setting themselves up just nicely for him to be noticed.

He looked over at the prisoners' hut where Leon Winters was right now lying in his own stink, too weak to work, just waiting on each minute to pass oh so slowly before the next one came along. Probably wondering if and when he was ever going to get out. As far as Webster knew, Winters had no idea yet what his old colleague Jim Jackson was planning. Well, he soon would. Once Jackson's plan failed, both of them would be in the system forever and it would be all down to Webster that the plan had been foiled.

He smiled. There ought to be a posting back to a more civilised camp after this. Maybe even the penitentiary back at Huntsville or Rusk. Might even be able to persuade his wife to come back to him if he was in a place like that. But there again, did he want her back?

On the other hand, it would be nice to stay here for just a little while – or wherever they were going to send Leon Winters and Jim Jackson after their failed escape-come-rescue attempt. Yes, he'd sure like to spend a few weeks with those two.

The sky was darker now. The faint stars were shining brighter.

Webster T. Ellington cracked his knuckles, spat tobacco juice on to the ground and started at the huts.

Tomorrow, maybe? The day after?

It didn't matter. The feeling was so good that in one way he wanted it to last a long time.

But not as much as he wanted to look into Jim Jackson's eyes again.

Red Kelly reckoned that it wasn't until he finished his third glass of beer that he'd rid himself of all the grit that a half-day's riding had deposited in his throat.

'This place is way too dry and dusty,' he said. 'Once we've

killed Jackson I want to find myself someplace cool and green again.'

'We need to find Jackson first,' Callum Short said.

'We will.'

'Well, let's hope we don't have to spend a day riding round again,' Ned Donovan said. His wounds still showed no signs of healing. Spending the afternoon on horseback up by the lumber camp had re-opened many of the pellet holes. By the time they'd risen and eaten breakfast it had been late morning and they'd missed the opportunity to watch the hotel for any fellow that might be Jim Jackson. So they'd taken some directions from the hotel clerk and had ridden up to the camp where this Jackson fellow was supposedly heading. They hadn't found Jackson up there and the camp looked kind of quiet and normal – no excitement at all. So they'd wound their way back to Prairie City and a few beers to wash away the dust.

Red said, 'The hotel clerk says there's a fellow he reckons might be the one. He'll send a boy over to tell me when the fellow comes back.'

'Let's hope it's Jackson,' Ned said.

'It will be,' Red said. 'Sooner or later it will be.'

Jim Jackson tried to recall something that could only be known to Leon and himself. Something Leon would read and know it was genuine and not a trap.

He lay on the bed and thought back over the things they had done together, the train robberies and the nights drinking whiskey and counting proceeds. Sitting on porches talking about the future. The shared tales of their pasts, the people they had left behind and the ones they wanted to see again.

He remembered one night telling Leon about Jennifer, about how rich her father was, about how he had come west to make a quick fortune in order to be able to go back to Clark County, Illinois, with enough wealth to be worthy of her.

'How's that working out?' Leon had asked him at the time.

'I'd say I'm on track,' Jim had said.

Leon had smiled a wide smile in the moonlight, with a bottle of wine between them on the wooden steps on which they sat.

'Well, don't stay in this game too long, my friend. Once you've made enough, be gone. *Carpe diem*, and all that.'

'*Carpe diem?*'

'Seize the day. It's Latin. It's Italian. I don't know. Might be Shakespeare. What I do know is that your luck mightn't last forever.'

'You know Shakespeare?' Jim had asked Leon that night.

'Some. You? Do you read?'

And their friendship, already strong, had become even stronger.

Now, sitting in his darkening hotel room, Jim Jackson wrote in his neatest and clearest writing – making sure the lettering was large enough for a man to read even if his eyesight was no longer what it once was – instructions for what he wanted Leon to do the day after he had received the note. He ended with: 'My luck – like yours – didn't last for ever. But we have a chance to put it all right. *Carpe diem*.'

CHAPTER THIRTEEN

Somebody was hammering on the door.

They were all sleeping in the same room – although after today Red wasn't sure where they were going to bunk down. Money was just about up. It might be that they could rob someone but he really didn't want to risk bringing any attention to himself and the boys and it would defeat the entire purpose of being in Prairie City if they had to skip town. Maybe they'd have to bed down with the horses for a night or two. That was assuming they could afford the livery.

'Who the hell's that at this godforsaken hour?' Ned grumbled.

'It's morning,' Red said, untangling himself from his blanket. He ran a hand through his hair, grabbed his hat from the table at the end of the bed, and opened the door.

It was the clerk. Red had slipped him fifty cents the day before and told him that whenever and wherever he spotted a tall fellow on his own, who was new in town, to come and tell Red.

'There's a feller eating breakfast right now. Downstairs. Reckon it might be the feller you're looking for.'

Red, Callum, and Ned followed the clerk down the steep creaking stairs. He led them to the door that opened on to the breakfast room and indicated a man sitting on his own, eating fried bacon and eggs, and drinking coffee.

Red thought back to those few seconds in the carriage of the Austin-bound train. He had walked into the carriage and had seen Ringo lying on the floor, motionless, blood pouring from his head. Wes had been there too, as large as life, being held down in an armlock by some big young men. And beyond Wes was . . . this man. The tall man. Red hadn't recalled getting a good look at him but now it all came back. This man had had bloodlust in his eyes.

'It's him,' Red said.

There was something in Red's voice because the clerk said, 'I don't want no trouble. Not here. Not in the hotel.'

Red said, 'It's too late to avoid trouble now.' He turned to his two comrades. 'Boys, our guns. Come on.'

By the time Red had gone upstairs, strapped his gun on, and made it back down, Jim Jackson was on the street. But that was OK. Killing the man in the breakfast room mightn't have been a good idea. Too many other folks around. Red had his own neck to think about, too.

Jackson was walking slowly up Main Street. He paused once or twice to look into shop windows, and he smiled at several pretty ladies. He had a brown paper bag in his right hand and saddle-bags over his shoulder.

'Livery's where he's headed,' Ned said.

'Uh-huh.'

'It's quieter up there.'

'Uh-huh.'

Red was thinking the same thing. The livery was on the edge of town. Whilst Jackson was sorting his horse out, sad-dling her up and probably sweet-talking her, they could get a few hundred yards up the trail and be ready for him. It didn't have to take long. Shoot the horse. Walk on over, maybe put a bullet in Jackson's leg, just to quieten him down and stop him running, and then let him know just why he was being sent to Hell. Let him think about it for a few seconds, see the fear in his eyes, and then . . . bang.

'Ned: Callum and I will take care of Jackson. We'll sneak up the trail a little. You go into the stables you get our horses ready. We're going to need to get away quickly after we've killed him.'

'He killed Ringo,' Ned said. 'I'd like to see—'

'I know,' Red said, his voice a little softer than normal. 'And we'll make sure he knows that's why we're here. But we need those horses ready. You go on ahead, Ned. Get there before Jackson if you can and make a start on those horses. Go on. Get ahead of him.'

Ned grunted but picked up his speed, limping slightly as he pulled away from Red and Callum.

Over on the other side of the street, Jackson stopped to say something to a young man brewing and selling coffee. The young man smiled and nodded. Jackson set off again. A short-haired brown dog stood up and followed him for a few paces. Jackson said something to the dog and its tail twitched briefly.

Callum said, 'Boss, it might be nothing. But. . . '

'But what?'

'There's a fellow about twenty yards behind Jackson. Black coat with a yellow vest beneath. Bearded fellow.'

'I see him.'

'I think he's following Jackson, too.'

Ben Adams was weary. That was the thing with trying to watch a man, you had to be on your wits all of the time. The fellow in question could sleep, and he could take a long leisurely breakfast, and he could drink his coffee whilst sitting down, and meanwhile you had to be up early, grabbing your food and drink on the go – if at all – and you couldn't even take a break to relieve yourself. It was exhausting. The tiredness was making him a little short-tempered – he'd cursed the hotel clerk for no reason earlier – and it was causing him to make mistakes. Earlier he'd found his eyes closing briefly in the warm morning sun, just as Jackson emerged from the hotel, well fed and rested. At least George Dubois up at the stables would pick him up if Adams missed him. But that wasn't the point. Adams hated making mistakes.

Still, all the grit in his eyes, the hunger in his belly and even the uncomfortable pressure in his bladder would be worth it in the end, when they were right there when Jackson broke his old partner out of the prison camp. To see the look in the man's eyes – both men's eyes – and to get the plaudits back in Austin when he brought the train robber in. Yes, it would be worth it then. It was a shame that Higgs wouldn't be there to see it, but hell, what a negotiating position it would give him with whoever the new boss was.

He followed Jackson at a fair distance and in his tiredness it was a few minutes before he realized that he wasn't the only one following the train robber.

There were two of them.

Scruffy, dirty trail-hands by the look of them. Stubble on their faces and dust on their coats and chaps and boots.

Adams cursed his own tiredness. He should have spotted these two right away.

Then they both turned and looked directly at him.

'Sonofabitch,' Red said. 'Who the hell's that?'

'Never seen him before,' Callum said.

'No way on God's earth that fellow is taking Jackson away from me. Jackson is mine.'

They were getting closer to the livery.

'You want me to stop him?' Callum reached down and loosened the Colt in his holster. It had been a while since he had used the gun. He wouldn't have minded shooting someone, especially someone who was trying to prevent them getting justice for Little Joe and Ringo, and no doubt Wes and Lech too.

'Let me think,' Red said.

'Up ahead,' Callum said. 'The livery entrance is around that corner and down a way. We'll get there first. Jackson will be inside the livery. Ned will follow him if needs be and we'll catch up later. You and I can wait on this feller.'

Red looked up the street. Yes, that would work. Surprise the fellow as he came round the corner.

'You got a knife?'

'Nope. Just a gun.'

'I've got a knife,' Red said.

'You going to kill him?'

'I don't know. Maybe I'll just ask him who he is.'

Adams couldn't figure it. Who else would be trailing Jackson? Maybe he'd upset someone in town? He'd got plenty drunk enough. But these two . . . they looked like they ridden a hundred miles to get here. How would they know that Jackson would be here right now?

He'd have to ask them. Simple as that. Neither looked like they had much about themselves. He couldn't risk them messing things up.

Damn it.

Jackson was almost at the livery now. He turned a corner and was out of sight – but that was OK, since George would be picking him up in a moment.

A few seconds later and the two fellows went around the corner, too.

Adams raised his pace.

Adams came round the corner and one of the men was waiting for him. The fellow grabbed Adams' arm and spun him round, smashing his head up against the wooden wall of the livery stable. For a moment Adams' vision wavered. Pain erupted from his shoulder blades where they had hit the hard wood.

As the pain flared out he tensed his stomach muscles, expecting the man to punch him in the belly. That's what he would have done.

But instead the fellow let go of his wrist and stepped closer.

Adams blinked, clearing his vision, and now the man was pressing a knife to his throat. The man's breath was foul. The stubble on his face was light brown, almost red. His teeth were coffee-coloured.

'Who in the hell are you?' the man said.

The fellow pressed the knife hard enough against his throat that Adams felt the skin give way and blood trickle down.

The second man was standing behind the first. He had his gun drawn.

'Name's Ben Adams.'

'Yeah, but *who* are you?'

'What do you want with Jackson?' This was the second man, darker hair and bloodshot eyes, dust in his beard.

So they knew Jackson's name.

'Who's Jackson?' Adams said.

'The fellow you were following.'

'I'm not following anyone.'

The red-haired man pressed the knife deeper into Adams' throat.

'He's mine, you understand? You turn around and walk back the way you came.'

'Who are you?'

'That don't matter.'

'It matters to me.'

Across the street a woman and a man had paused and were watching what was happening. A fellow was over there standing in a doorway, also looking on.

Behind the second man, the one with his gun drawn, Adams saw George Dubois come into view.

Time to take control of the situation and make these fellows pay for drawing a knife on him.

He turned his head slightly to the left, easing the pressure against the blade, and at exactly the same moment he drove his right fist hard into the red-haired man's side. The man's eyes widened and evil-smelling breath exploded from his lungs. He doubled over. Adams twisted away from the wall and brought a knee up smashing it into the man's jaw.

The one with the gun said 'Jesus' and started to raise his gun, but George was there pressing his own revolver against the fellow's neck, telling him to stay still and not to move a muscle. The man paused, his gun still pointing at the ground.

'Drop the gun,' George said.

Now Adams kicked the red-haired man's legs backward and the fellow, still gasping for breath, crumpled to the floor. Adams stamped on the man's knife hand, and the man let go of the knife.

The other man dropped his gun.

Adams sensed there were more people watching now, a growing crowd. He knelt down beside Red and grabbed the man's hand, twisted it in such a way that the man actually squealed, a strange pig-like sound as the pain and the need to breathe got all tangled up in his throat. Then he had hold of the man's middle finger, bending it back.

'Your turn,' Adams said. 'Who are you? Why are you following Jackson?'

Red didn't know that such pain was contained within his fingers. The fellow was doing something to his hand that made it feel like a knife was being drawn slowly and deeply along his entire arm, into his shoulder, up his neck and into his brain. He couldn't breathe, either. He needed air to help with the pain but the fellow's punch felt like it had crushed his insides.

It was wrong. *He* was the one who had been in control and in a heartbeat he was on belly, face down in the dirt, and the pain was so bad that he could actually feel urine dribbling into his pants and he was helpless to do anything about it.

Where was Cal?

Cal should have been there behind him, with a gun. There were two of them. One of this fellow. It was wrong.

Now the man bent his finger back so far that there was a sound like a dry branch snapping and all the pain that had gone before was nothing. This was like a sheet of white fire that filled his whole body. Air or no air, he couldn't help but scream.

Ned Donovan was crouched beneath Red's horse trying to buckle up a saddle strap when he heard the scream. It was Red. He didn't know how he knew, he just did. He'd heard Red yell a few times when they were riding alongside a train or chasing down a lone rider. But he'd never heard Red scream and yet he knew this was Red. It was an awful scream, a scream full of pain and anguish.

Ned stood up.

Across the livery, in another stall, Jackson stood up too. He'd no doubt heard it too. He looked over at Ned. It felt strange to have the man they had been tracking down staring right at him, blissfully unaware of what they were planning to do. For a moment Ned felt sure that Jackson could read his mind.

But then came another scream and this one made Ned reach down and slip his gun from his holster, and without another look at Jackson he ran outside.

When Ben Adams snapped the fellow's second finger, George knew the man was about to start talking. He was weeping now.

'Don't move,' George said to the one he was standing next to, his gun still pressed into the man's neck.

'Let him be,' the man said. He was trembling.

'Who are you?' Adams asked the fellow on the ground. 'Why are you following Jackson?

The man took a great gulp of air and tried to stop the sobs in his throat long enough to speak, quickly enough to stop another finger being snapped.

But before he could say anything another man stepped out of the livery. This one was equally dirty and unkempt, his clothes dusty, his face bearded.

And this one had a gun in his hand.

This one was raising his gun.

This one's finger whitened as he started to squeeze the trigger.

George twisted, moving the barrel of his own gun from the back of the man's neck in front of him, and lined up on the new fellow.

George shot him.

Jim Jackson heard the scream and turned just in time to see another fellow standing up in a stall. They looked at one another and Jim pulled a face as if to say *what's going on?* The man stared at him. He looked scared, and when there was a second scream the man drew his gun and rushed outside.

A moment later there was a gunshot, followed by a brief silence, and then the sound of a lady crying and men shouting, and beneath that another man swearing.

The temptation was to take a look at what was going on. Gunshots and screaming weren't good, yet no man could fail to have his curiosity roused by them. Nevertheless, he'd been witness to more than enough of both over the years, and today wasn't a day to be getting pulled into the petty, if vicious, squabbles of Prairie City. Today was a day to be sticking to his plan.

So he finished saddling up his mare, and then he rode her outside, turned away from the crowd and headed into the hills.

The sheriff's name was Tom August. 'Like the month,' he'd said to Ben Adams, a cocked shotgun in his hands pointing right at Adams' belly. August had been across the street when the commotion had started. If it had just been a fight he may have left them to it, but when he heard the gunshot he had snapped that shotgun into readiness and had strode across the street. He saw that, in addition to the three standing men, there was a fellow dead in the dirt, and another on the floor with his hand tucked beneath his armpit and a look in his eyes like he wanted to burn the whole town down.

'What a Godforsaken mess,' August said.

'I'm Ben Adams, trouble-shooter for the Houston and Texas. I need to speak to you in private urgently,' one of the men said.

'Do you now?'

'It's important.'

'I'm sure it is.'

'Can we talk?'

'The Houston and Texas, huh?'

'Yes.'

'I'll check it out.'

'We need to talk—'

'What we need to do is to get Bones to have a look at this man's hand, and we need to get this poor fellow covered up—'

'It's urgent!'

'Then I need to talk to a few people, see if I can't ascertain what happened.' The sheriff looked around, registering the faces of those people who had witnessed events.

'I figure the first thing, though, is you,' he nodded at the man who still had a smoking gun in his hand. 'You give your gun to. . . .' He looked around the crowd again. 'You give your gun to Louis.' He nodded at a tall man in the crowd. The tall man nodded back. 'Louis, you pick up that other gun that's on the floor, too. Martin,' he looked at another crowd member. 'You go and knock Bones up – he's probably still asleep – and tell him to get over to my office. And Maria, can you call on Skater and ask him to come and do something decent with this dead man.' A woman in the crowd smiled and nodded.

He turned back to Adams.

'Trouble-shooter, huh?'

'Yes.'

'Looks to me like you might be a trouble-causer. We'll get to the bottom of this mess, you can be sure of that. Meanwhile I'm afraid to say I'm going to have to lock all of you boys up.'

'No.'

'I'm afraid so. Now all of you, you walk in front of Louis and me. Any trouble and I'll shoot you. I mean it. I hate paperwork and would you believe there's less for a dead man than for a darn investigation. Come on. Move. I've got two cages and luckily they're both empty. Now walk.'

CHAPTER FOURTEEN

Jim Jackson knelt at the edge of the tree line and whistled quietly. Too quietly – neither the boy nor dog heard him. They were too far away, over by the big brick house. The boy was wandering around with a stick, throwing it every once in a while for the dog to retrieve, but most of the time pushing it into the ground, turning over rocks with it, sometimes crouching down to see what he had uncovered.

Jim had circled the camp when he had first arrived. It was quiet, as it had been these last few days: almost deserted, just the one guard spending most of his time leaning on the gate.

It struck Jim that his plan was too complex, that it was full of holes. It would have been easier to just to have ridden into the camp with a shotgun in one hand, a six-gun in the other, and taken Leon in full view of the guard. And if the guard had put up a fight. . . . Well, so be it. That way would have worked. It was probably more liable to work than his current plan. But it still might have meant shooting dead the guard. The alarm would go up and they – the remaining guards, and whatever posse they could raise – would be on his and Leon's tail quicker than if he did this thing surreptitiously.

It might yet come to plan B. But this place never changed day to day, so he'd try it the quiet way first.

He had picked a position where what gentle breeze there was blew over his shoulder. The skinned rabbit he had bought the day before in Prairie City was at his feet.

He whistled again, louder. This time the terrier stopped mid-step, a front paw raised in the air, its head cocked to one side and its ears pointing up.

Jim reached down and picked up the rabbit carcass. He couldn't smell it, but he hoped the terrier could.

Another whistle.

Now the dog saw him.

Its nose twitched and its tail wagged. It barked, looked once at the boy, and then came running towards him. It was within ten yards of him when the boy called.

'Blue! Here boy.'

The dog skidded on the dry dusty ground. It stopped but didn't turn. Instead it stood looking at Jim Jackson, tail wagging, its tongue flicking out and moistening its nose.

The boy looked over.

'Rabbit?' Jim said, reaching down, picking up the carcass and holding it out.

'Blue!'

The dog's nose twitched faster. But it didn't move.

Now the boy was walking towards them.

The boy saw Jim.

The boy opened his mouth to yell.

'It's all right,' Jim said. 'It's all right.' He dropped the rabbit and held up his hands in mock surrender. 'I'm a friend.'

The boy stood there for a moment, his mouth still open.

Then the dog shot forward and grabbed the rabbit carcass, turned and ran, taking the meat to a safe distance.

Jim smiled. 'It's OK. I brought it for him.'

The boy's mouth closed. Then opened again and he said, 'Who are you?'

'My name is Jim. What's yours?'

'You said you were a friend.'

'I am.'

'I don't know you. How can you be my friend?'

About twenty yards beyond the boy, the terrier was tearing at the rabbit carcass.

'I brought your dog a rabbit.'

'He can catch his own.'

'Not many rabbits about this time of day.'

'Are you hiding?'

'No.'

'Then why are you crouched down in the trees?'

'Well, maybe I am hiding. Just a little. You like secrets?'

'Uh-huh. I guess.'

'Can you keep a secret?'

'Yes.'

'How can I be sure?'

'I can keep one. Besides, there ain't no one to tell a secret to. Only Billy.

'Who's Billy?'

'He guards the gate. He's new.'

'If I tell you a secret you won't tell Billy, will you?'

'No.'

'Promise?'

'Cross my heart and hope to die.'

'OK. What's your name, son?'

'Alfie.'

'How old are you, Alfie?'

'I'm six.'

'OK, Alfie, I'm going to trust you.'

Whilst speaking, Jim had pulled the telescope from the inside of his jacket.

'Wow, what's that? An eye-glass?'

'This? This is a telescope. It belonged to a soldier in the war. A general.'

'What war?'

'The war between the States.'

'Can I see?'

Jim handed the telescope to Alfie. He then knelt down next

to the boy and showed him how to use it.

'That's amazing!' Alfie said.

'Listen,' Jim said. 'Do you know LT?'

'LT?'

'Leon.'

'The only one I know is Billy.'

'Leon is a tall man. He's in the shed. The shed for men who can't work.'

'Oh, the tall man.'

'Yes.'

'He's a dead man walking. That's what Billy says.'

The words made Jim go cold. His throat was suddenly dry. He swallowed.

'I'm sure he is,' Jim said. 'But here's my secret. I'm an old friend of Leon's.'

'You are?'

'Yes. And because he's a dead man walking I'd like to get a final message to him. Just to say goodbye. Can you understand that?'

'I guess so.'

'Can you read, Billy?'

'A little.'

'Well, you don't need to read anything, just pass a message to Leon.'

'I never talk to him. Not to any of them.'

'I know. But sometimes you fill up the outhouse with paper.'

'It smells!'

'I'm sure it does.'

'How about the next time you see Leon go into the out-house, you run in and give him some outhouse paper. Could you do that?'

'I guess so.'

'But you mustn't tell anyone. Not anyone. Not even Billy.'

'OK.'

'I'll give you some special paper.'

'I'll need to get Billy to open the gate.'

'Who usually gives you the outhouse paper?'

'There's a pile in the storeroom. I do it every day.'

'You done it today?'

'Not yet.'

'Then Billy will let you through?'

'Yeah.'

'OK. Here's the paper. You don't need to read it. Tell Leon that Jim sent it. And Alfie. . . .'

'Yes?'

'If you do this and if you keep this secret and don't tell anyone then tomorrow I'll give you the telescope.'

'You will?'

'I will.'

'I promise. Cross my heart and hope to die!'

Whittaker Gordon said to Billy Burke, 'Is that Leon Winters?'

'Yes, that's him,' Billy said.

Billy was pleased to have the railroad guard with him. He hadn't realized how lonely he had become in this job. Whilst the others rode off every day and watched over the men as they worked the timber, no doubt talking and laughing and sharing stories, he was here on his own, keeping a watch on a few weak men who could hardly raise themselves off their beds, let alone raise any trouble. Captain Fisher came down once in a while and had a chat, asked how Billy was getting on, but those conversations only lasted a few minutes and then the captain was off doing his rounds. Most of the time, though, the captain was up at the house or even away altogether. Billy wasn't sure if Fisher didn't own part of the business that all these men cut the lumber for. Then there was Webb Ellington. Webb was around a fair bit, too, though some days he went off with the gang. But he tended to keep himself to himself and when they did talk he was mostly grumpy and depressing, until these last few days when Webster had bucked up a bit.

'Doesn't look much,' Whit said.

'He ain't been eating. Got a sickness or something. It's been going round. He was thin to start with.'

The captain had brought Whit down yesterday and introduced him to Billy. Said a team of railroad men from Austin were watching out for someone and wanted to place a man in the camp for a day or two. Billy was to look after Whit, find him a bunk, some food, and so on.

'He been here a long time?'

'Longer than me.'

'How long you been here?'

'Couple of months. But most of the men been here years.'

Leon Winter shuffled very slowly towards the outhouse. As he walked he held up his trousers with one hand to stop them slipping down his bony frame.

'Billy! Billy!'

Billy turned. Behind them little Alfie skidded to a halt, his dog at his feet.

'I ain't done the paper. I forgot. Blue caught a rabbit.'

Billy wasn't sure whether the rabbit was the reason Alfie had forgot to load up the paper stack or an unrelated piece of news.

'Well, best you get on over there quickly before Winters stinks up the place. You run fast enough you'll catch him before he gets there.'

Billy opened the gate and Alfie ran through, a thick sheaf of paper squares in his hand.

As Leon Winters reached for the outhouse door handle he heard a young voice breathlessly call his name from behind.

He turned.

It was the kid. He'd seen the boy many a time, running around outside the fence with his dog at his heels. Always smiling. Too young yet to know how the world can turn on you.

But the kid had never said anything to him before, let alone called him by his name. Hell, how would the kid even know his name?

'Leon,' the kid said again, as if he was enjoying the moment, enjoying being allowed to say a prisoner's name.

'Hello,' Leon said, and even smiled. It wasn't the kid's fault that, out of anyplace in the world he could have grown up, God had dumped him in this one.

'Paper,' the boy said, holding out a thick wad of outhouse paper squares.

'Thank you,' Leon said, still puzzling on how the boy had known his name.

The boy grinned and turned to go. Then he said, 'Jim sent it.'

Billy and Whit watched Alfie hand Leon Winters the toilet paper, then turn and run back towards them.

The kid was smiling. Hell, the kid was always smiling.

Billy opened the gate and let Alfie out.

'Got there before the stink,' Billy said.

Alfie smiled. He went through the gate, turned and said, 'I'm getting a telescope.'

Then he was gone, running up to the big house, dog racing round his heels.

'Kid seems a bit simple to me,' Whit said.

'He's just young,' Billy said.

Leon closed the door. The wood had warped and cracked over the years. The door squeaked and moaned and thin shafts of dusty sunlight came through the gaps.

His hands were trembling.

Had the boy really said what Leon thought he'd said?

Jim sent it.

All those years. The endless years. The tortures, both physical and mental, the hopelessness and the despair. The knowing that you were alone and that *this* was it, forever. That one way or another you were never going to be free again. Sometimes wanting to end it all. Other times fighting back. But always hanging on to something, some knowledge or hope that one day something would happen.

Jim sent it.

Leon looked at the paper in his hand. It was just paper. But it was paper Jim had sent.

There'd only been one Jim. Jim Jackson: his best friend in the old gang. Leon recalled nights spent talking, looking at the stars, discussing books. Jim Jackson had no more been a train robber than he'd been a whale hunter. He did it for love. For money, sure. But love was behind the money. Yet he turned out to be good at it in his own unique gentlemanly way. Leon tried to recall the last time they'd spoke. There been all that fighting – not he and Jim, the two of them had trusted each other – but all of them arguing and cussing and trying to work out who had shot that Texas Ranger on the train. They all had masks on and in the confusion no one could be sure who did it. Or why. That had been the end of it. The end of the good times. The beginning of the hell. But it hadn't been the last time. There had been other times, sad times. A goodbye. He recalled Jim riding off, saying he was done. Heading for home to get his few things together and then aiming back east to see if that love that he'd gone through everything for was still there. That had been the last time.

Leon didn't want to put the paper down, so he dropped his trousers one-handed – they just slid down over his hips without help anyway – and he sat over the hole in the wooden plank and he looked at the paper in his hand.

The first sheet was blank.

The second had writing on it but it was too dark to make out the words.

His stomach gurgled and below him he heard the gentle

flow of the creek.

He held the paper up so the shaft of light coming through the gap between door and wall lit it up.

He read.

At first he wondered if it was a trap. An elaborate trap. They did that sometimes – tried to entice a man into running. Just so they could have fun hunting him down, watching his sudden hope slowly ebb away and turn to despair. Then they'd shoot him.

They'd tried numerous times to drive Leon to escape. Maybe more times than the other men. It was as if, for some reason, they wanted him dead more than they wanted anyone else dead.

But would they go to these lengths? Would they have gone so far as to employ the kid in such a ruse?

Yes, he figured. Yes they would.

Then, at the bottom of the note, the writing said: 'My luck – like yours – didn't last for ever. But we have a chance to put it all right. *Carpe diem.*'

His heart raced. His stomach tightened and the gurgling stopped.

It was from Jim.

It had to be.

He read the words again. And he was convinced.

Jim sent it.

Jim Jackson eased back into the trees. The kid had done well. And when Leon had emerged from the outhouse he had, quite surreptitiously, looked up and around the hills surrounding the camp.

Now Jim circled the camp on the horse, taking his time, listening, and being more careful than ever.

He left the horse high in the trees above the timber yard and he worked his way down to the piles of lumber on foot. He chose two piles where the great logs looked dry and ready to burn, and where there were gaps and holes he could put his small bags of shotgun powder, shells and home-made fuses.

He memorised where he had put the incendiary devices and then he worked his way back to his horse.

Tomorrow was the day.

Red was mad. Drunk and mad.

First Little Joe. Then Ringo. Now Ned. Add in Wes and Lech – because they were as good as dead – and that meant almost all of the gang. Someone – *several people* – were going to pay. Jackson for killing his little brother. And that railroad fellow, Adams, for breaking his fingers – God, that had hurt. Not just when the man had done it, but when the doctor had snapped them back into place as well. His fingers were bound up now, splinted with little sticks and tight bandages and the whiskey helped ease the pain. In a way that pain was good. It made him mad and even more determined. But it didn't end there. The one that was called George had to die too. He'd shot poor Ned in cold blood. Right there in the street. How in the hell that yellow-bellied sheriff had come to release George and Adams, Red couldn't figure. It was cold-blooded murder, plain as day. But that was the thing, wasn't it? That was always the thing. The men turned out to be some railroad employees, investigators or something. They were all in it together. Sheriffs and detectives, the whole lot of them. Well, they'd get what was coming to them.

It was almost dusk before Sheriff August had finally uncaged them.

'This is the deal,' August had said. 'I'm letting you go. But there's a condition. The condition is you get your belongings, you take your horses, and you leave town.'

'We didn't do nothing,' Red argued. 'It was my man that got shot dead. Murdered.'

'I've spoken to all the witnesses. You leave. That's the deal. I'll walk with you over to the hotel. You collect your stuff and then we'll go to the stables and I watch you leave. It's too hot for me to sit here writing up paperwork, but if you don't like the deal then that's what I'll do. You can stay in the cage for a week, a month, however long it takes before I figure out what to do with you. Is it a deal?'

At least the sheriff had let Red spend the last of his money on a bottle of rotgut whiskey before leaving town. 'My fingers hurt like hell,' Red had said. 'If you ain't charging the man that broke them, at least let me get something to dull the pain.'

Now he and Callum were holed up in the woods about three miles north of Prairie City, not far off the trail that led up to the lumber camp. They had whiskey in their bellies against the pain and blankets around their shoulders against the cold, blankets that Red had stolen right from under the nose of that sheriff whilst they had been collecting their few things from the hotel. The worse thing was that when Red had been coming out of the hotel, August right by his side, there had been Jackson sitting in the eating room with a big plate of bread and beans.

'It ain't over,' Red slurred now. 'I'll bet money, if I had any, that tomorrow Jackson will be riding up this very trail, and not far behind will be those railroad men.'

'And we'll be behind *them*,' Callum said.

'We'll be behind them,' Red agreed.

CHAPTER FIFTEEN

There was a knot in Jim Jackson's belly. It felt like that hot rock of fear that he had been carrying for several days ever since seeing Captain Ellington up at the camp. Although this knot was made up of excitement and anticipation as well as fear. It was the same feeling he'd had all those years back when embarking on a train robbery. There was knowledge that it could be a good day, when everything might go according to plan, and the rewards would be wonderful. But the other side of the nickel was always the very real possibility that if things didn't go as planned then the results could be terrible.

Today the stakes were higher than ever.

By the time it was over he and Leon might be riding together again, free after all of this time. There'd be a period of catching up, recovering, building strength, and explanations. But they'd be riding side-by-side just like the old days. And this time it would be revenge rather than riches they were riding towards.

Or. . . .

By nightfall he might be dead. Maybe worse. By nightfall he might be in the clutches of the Texas system again; the Texas system as personified by Captain Ellington. The thought was paralysing. That knot, that hot rock, suddenly tightening, making him dizzy with fear.

He wiped perspiration from his forehead. The taste of bile was strong in his mouth. He closed his eyes and breathed deeply, letting the oxygen clear his throat, his lungs, his blood. He exhaled slowly, calming himself.

Then he adjusted and tightened his gun belt and put a box of Lucifers in his pocket.

He stepped outside.

Adams and Dubois were already saddled up and waiting in a copse of pine trees just north of the Prairie City boundary line. There were no chances to be had this morning. They'd failed to follow Jim Jackson for two days. Sooner or later he was going to do what he came for and they couldn't afford to miss him again, even with Whit stationed up at the lumber camp.

'August tell you anything more about those other fellows?' Dubois said. He was rolling a cigarette as he sat waiting on his horse.

'I don't want you lighting that,' Adams said. 'I'd like a cigarette myself but if the wind is right you can smell a man smoking even if you can't see him.'

'OK, boss.'

'To answer your question, no. August seemed to think they had something to hide. I tend to agree. But they never said anything all the time he had them locked up. I mean, they talked: August said they moaned and wanted to know if we were going to be charged – me for breaking his fingers and you for killing that fellow. August said they ate like they hadn't eaten for days, too.'

'You think they've gone?'

'Yeah. I hurt the red-haired one bad. You hear how he screamed? Like a stuck piglet. And the fact you shot one of them—'

'I've never killed anyone before.'

Adams looked over at the young man. Tree branches and the man's hat shadowed his face. It was impossible to see

Dubois' eyes.

'You did well. Are you all right?'

They'd spoken about it yesterday, locked up in a storeroom at the sheriff's office. August hadn't put them in the second cage on account of it sharing a set of bars with the cage in which he'd locked Red and the other fellow, whose name turned out to be Callum. But the sheriff had locked them up nonetheless. 'Just for a few hours,' he'd said. 'Whilst I wire your railroad.' In that storeroom, dark, oppressive and hot, George Dubois had said, initially, that he was OK about killing a man, especially as the fellow was pointing a gun at him. But as the hours had passed he had grown quieter, only occasionally saying things such as, 'You think he had a brother? A sister?' and later, 'You think his parents are still alive? You think they know where he is?' Adams had reassured Dubois that what he'd done was the right thing, not just for that moment that they had found themselves in, but beyond that too. A man intent upon killing another man in cold blood was not a good man. Sooner or later he would go through with a killing. Maybe more than one. In the eyes of the law, and even in the eyes of God, Adams said, what George had done has been the *only* thing to do.

'Yeah, I think I'm all right,' George said now.

Adams breathed in. There was freshness to the air, the smell of leaves and grass on the slight wind.

'We all get to kill a man for the first time one day,' he said. 'After that it gets easier.'

The boy looked so similar to little Alfie up at the lumber camp that when he handed Jim the note Jim had to do a double take. The same age, the same height, even the same tousled hair. If this boy had had a dog circling his feet then Jim would have really wondered if he wasn't imagining things.

'The lady told me to give you this,' the boy said, smiling. 'She was real pretty.' Then he ran off.

The lady?

Jim looked up and down Main Street. It was as it had always been since he had arrived here a few days ago – quiet compared to Austin, but lively in its own way: folks walking up and down on their way somewhere, but that somewhere not immediately apparent. Horses, carts, horses and carts, fellows unloading boxes, fellows carrying boxes, dogs scratching in the shadows, the smell of fire and smoke as the coffee-boy boiled water and unseen folks cooked breakfast, a few trail hands leaning against posts and a few pretty women on the plank-walks . . . but none of them looking his way or paying him any attention.

He glanced down at the paper in his hand. It was folded in two. He opened it and a shiver ran all the way up his spine and out through his shoulders. Then came warmth, flooding through him even before he'd read any words. He could hear – or feel – his own heartbeat, the blood rushing through his ears. He'd seen that writing before, that neat script, the straight clean lines.

It was Rosalie's writing.

He read the note.

I'm in the church. Come immediately. But don't be followed. They know you're here.

What?

He read it again, trying to understand it.

Rosalie was here? In Prairie City? Why? How?

Who were 'they'?

And how did they know he was here?

Too many questions, too much confusion. Thoughts crashed and ricocheted inside his head.

He looked up and down Main Street again. The coffee-boy saw him and waved. He waved back, the gesture automatic.

There was no question but to go to the church. Unless . . . he wondered could it be a trap? But why? And who? No, he had to go – this was most definitely Rosalie's beautiful writing

115

and now he realized how much he longed to see her, how much he had missed her, and how hard he'd had to struggle to keep such emotions locked away because he'd genuinely believed he would never see her again.

But time was tight. He had to get up to the camp and hide away in the copse with the extra horse he'd already arranged over at the livery. Be there for Leon. However it turned out.

He folded the letter, and thrust it into a pocket. Then he turned and walked in the opposite direction to the church, stopping at random intervals, turning, trying to see if anyone in this quiet town a hundred miles from Austin was following him.

The church interior was dark, save for dusty lines of light shining through the small windows high on either side. The aromas of old incense and newly sawn wood floated in the still air. At the head of the church a simple wooden cross stood on a plain altar. Unlit candles were positioned either side of it.

He stood in the open doorway and the low morning sun cast a long shadow of his body on the floor before him.

'Close the door,' she said, from the darkness somewhere to the left.

Her voice made him smile and tremble. He felt hot and scared simultaneously.

He turned towards her voice but couldn't see her.

'Rosalie?'

'The door.'

He turned and pushed the door closed, and when he turned back she was there, coming out of the shadows, grabbing him, holding him, hugging him. She was crying and she was laughing and she knocked his hat off and he kissed her hair.

'I never thought I'd see you again,' she said, looking up at him now, her eyes wet with tears and even prettier than he remembered. She laughed and it turned into a sob. He kissed

116

her hair again and tasted sand and dirt. The trail grit was on her face, too. He held her at arm's length, looking at her, still smiling, but seeing how tired she was.

'Rosalie,' he said. 'How? Why?'

She stepped backwards and he allowed his fingers to slip along her arms, over her wrists, and when he held her fingers she cried in pain.

He looked down and saw that one hand was roughly splinted and bandaged.

'What happened? Who did this?'

'It was . . .' Tears rolled down her cheek as she remembered.

He held her again. 'It's OK,' he said.

'He followed us. After our meal. I should have let you walk me home.'

'Who? Tell me.'

They sat in a pew in the darkest corner of the church, and she told him how the man had forced her inside a deserted building and had broken two fingers, and how she had told him all she knew about Jim Jackson. She told how, afterwards, the man had left her sobbing in a doorway on the street and how she had somehow made it home, where Roberta had helped splint and fix the fingers and had told her off and comforted her in equal measures.

'Who was this man?'

'He said he was one of the good guys.'

She described the man as best she could, his dark stone-like eyes, his beard, and especially the quiet voice that somehow still felt loud and strong and chilling.

'I'll kill him,' Jim Jackson said, his own voice quiet. 'I mean it.'

'Roberta will kill me. I couldn't do anything the first few days. I just hurt so much. Not just my fingers. But inside. Everything. But I knew I had to come and find you and warn you. Tell you what I'd done.'

'You didn't do anything.'

'I told him all about you. I'm so sorry.'

'It's all right. Anyone would have.'

'No, it's not all right. So when Roberta was at work I arranged a horse and some food and I just . . . I just set out. I left her a note and I just rode. It was crazy. I got lost. I slept in the woods two nights.'

'You shouldn't have come.'

'And you would never have known that they're here. Watching you. Waiting.'

He held her. He kissed her sandy hair and when she looked up at him, the tears magnifying her beautiful eyes, he kissed her on the lips for the first time.

Leon Winters lay in bed and listened to the sound of his fellow prisoners marching out of camp, their footfalls becoming quieter as they walked away quickly.

Earlier, one of the guards had tried to get him to stand, telling him he'd been long enough in the sickbed and it was time to get back to work. Leon had stumbled deliberately, but he was still weak, and he wasn't sure himself how much of the stumble had been real.

'Let him be,' Webster Ellington had said. He'd been standing over at the door. 'Another day or two's rest won't hurt.'

The guard had looked at Ellington.

'You're getting soft. He's fit enough to carry water for the others.'

'Let him be.'

So Leon had lain back in bed, smelling the sweat and sickness that permeated the wooden floor and walls of the hut, feeling the temperature rise as the minutes ticked by. He watched spiders up there in the dark angles where the ceiling met the walls. He looked at the smeared finger and nose grease on the dirty windows. He listened to Harry across the room moan with every breath, his chest rattling and wheezing like a train engine that was about to expire.

You're getting soft.

It worried Leon. Webster Ellington was the cruellest of them all. He'd never shown an ounce of compassion before. Not once. Why all of a sudden did he not want Leon to be back out there with the gang?

On this day of all days.

But it was too late to worry about it.

At midday what would be would be.

'What are you going to do?' Rosalie asked.

'I have to be there at midday for him,' Jim said. 'Come what may.'

'But they'll be following you.'

'I can't leave him alone.'

'*I'll* do it.'

'What?'

'They're not following me. They don't even know I'm here.'

'No. You've been through enough. Look at you – you're exhausted. Your fingers. . . . No. That's crazy.'

'So you'll go up there anyway? Knowing that it's a trap. All I went through to get here – it's worth nothing?'

He looked at her, at her pretty eyes, at the stubbornness of her expression. She meant it.

'I didn't do all of this for nothing,' she said. 'Tell me. Where do I need to be? What do I need to do?'

'It's crazy.'

'Tell me.'

He told her.

CHAPTER SIXTEEN

'Wait,' Adams whispered. 'We know where he's going. There's no hurry.'

They watched Jim Jackson riding north, pushing his horse a little but not too hard.

'He looked a bit worried to me,' George Dubois said.

'He's been up and down every day. Maybe today's the day. He can't keep watching. Sooner or later he's got to act.'

The dust that Jackson's horse had kicked up had settled when the two railroad men eased their horses out of cover and started to follow.

'I've got a feeling in my bones,' Adams said. 'It's going to be a good day.'

Jim Jackson felt the sweat rise somewhere up between his shoulder blades and trickle down his back. It burned like an ice-cold blade and where the sweat settled in the small of his back it felt like a target.

He knew that they were out there somewhere. *They, he,* whomever. The one that had broken Rosalie's fingers. *Bastard.* He figured there'd be more than one. Maybe they were ahead of him. Maybe behind. Possibly both. He resisted the urge to look around. He didn't want them to know that he knew.

What he did was push his horse on. He had to assume that

they would be following him. He wanted to be a long way up the trail with them behind him by the time Rosalie came along.

'Just like I told you it would be,' Red said. 'First the one that shot my brother and then the one that broke my fingers. What did I tell you?'

Callum Short said, 'Yep. Exactly as you called it.'

'I should be a poker player. I can read men. I can read situations. Maybe that's what I'll do when all of this is over. I've seen 'em doing it in saloons. A good card player can make a fortune.'

They watched the two railroad men ride by, and when they were half a mile or so away they followed.

'I'd like to break his fingers before I kill him,' Red said. 'But I doubt I'll get the chance. Maybe if I can gut-shoot him first.'

'Don't take no chance though.'

'I won't. He's dangerous, I know that. He's quick like a snake. But then, once you know that, you can take steps to . . . you know, to accommodate what you know.'

'Yeah.'

'Like I said, I can read situations.'

Rosalie had watched Jim Jackson walk down the aisle and out of the church. He had smiled at the doorway, his face caught in a shaft of light from one of the windows, but once the door was open he didn't look back. She understood. He was being watched – but neither of them knew where the watchers were – so they had to play it careful. If anyone were observing him now they would likely assume that he'd just been saying a prayer. But even with that understanding, his leaving the church still felt too much like their parting moment back in Austin. There had been no looking back then. It was as if they were always fated to be walking away from one another.

She gave him plenty of time to reach the stables, saddle up, and leave town.

Then she followed.

Jim Jackson worked his way to the high ground above the camp. He'd told Leon that it would happen at noon. That at noon Leon should make his way to the outhouse and drop down into the creek. Follow it upwards, under the fence, and into the tree line. There will be a distraction, Jim had written.

It wasn't quite noon. There was still a morning shadow being cast by the whipping post standing in the yard.

But it was close.

Staying in the tree line, he circled the camp. His senses were heightened – the intense blue of the sky hurt his eyes. Had he ever really noticed the smell of the trees before? Or truly felt the caress of the gentle wind on his skin? Sounds, too. Birdsong, his horse's shoes on the stones and rocks, the rustle of dead leaves as she walked. It was as if life itself was pulling him closer, holding him tighter. He wondered if this was an omen.

Once or twice he thought he heard the snorting of distant horses. Imagination maybe? But at the same time he was hoping he was being followed. His plan had been turned upside down and twisted inside out. Now he had to draw the men away from the camp.

And after that? After that he would play it by ear. He would trust in his horse to be faster than theirs. Or his draw to be faster. Thinking about what the man had done to Rosalie's fingers he actually wondered if he would prefer the second option – instead of leading them clean away and avoiding the confrontation, maybe deep inside he actually wanted to look into the man's eyes and pull a trigger.

But no, that way would hold more risk. He needed to get back for Rosalie and for Leon.

He came down out of the trees, the horse slipping a little

on the scree.

The lumber piles were ahead of him. He urged his horse to move faster. A few minutes were all he needed. After that it was all about running and, hopefully, being chased.

The high sun told him noon was approaching. That whipping post shadow back in the yard would be gone.

He was here.

It was time.

He raced down into the gaps between the piles of lumber where only yesterday he had strategically hidden bags of gunpowder and shells and homemade fuses.

He leapt off his horse, pulled the box of Lucifers from his pocket, and ran to the first fuse.

He was breathing too fast. His hand was shaking. The first match slipped, unlit, from his nervous fingers. He forced himself to stop, take a deep breath, hold the air and then let it out through pursed lips.

Now try again. His thumbnail scratched a match into life and he lit the first fuse.

He ran along the pile of lumber and lit a second.

He whistled to his horse as he ran alongside the huge pile of lumber, lighting more fuses. The horse followed him.

When the first bag of powder went up it sounded initially like nothing more than the whistle of wind through the gap in a roof. He turned and looked back along the rows of piled up timber. There was a cloud of blue and grey smoke coming out from between two logs. A few flames too. But it was underwhelming. Doubt filled him. He needed to create something big that would be seen for miles. A little puff of smoke and some small flames would not be enough. Had he misjudged? Should he have found dynamite from somewhere?

A second bag of gunpowder went up.

Then several shotgun shells went off somewhere deep inside the log pile.

Another bag exploded.

This one was louder as if the confines of where he had buried it had magnified the explosion.

He leapt upon his horse and urged her forwards.

Somewhere behind he thought he heard shouting. More shotgun shells exploded and he could smell burning gunpowder in the air.

As the last bag of powder exploded he glanced back.

The smoke was rising upwards now, thickening already. Flames were licking around the outside of the log-pile. Through the smoke he could see two riders in the distance.

'Follow me,' he whispered. 'Follow me.'

It was midday.

Leon Winters felt livelier than he had in months, possibly years. He was weak, sure, but there was a different strength in him this morning. It didn't come from his muscles; it came from his heart. It was the strength of hope. It was energy that came from doing something, instead of being done to.

He stood on one of the bunks on the yard side of the hut, looking out through the dirty glass and watched the shadows shrink.

'You got the ... fidgets ... today, Leon?' Harry asked. Harry's breathing problem made it sound like he'd always just finished a mile-long run when he talked. Even when he wasn't talking there was a wheezing in his chest and throat as he tried to catch and hang on to each breath. His condition was worsening daily. When he could summon the energy to talk, Harry would often say that this was it. He was going to die in this stinking hot hut that even the rats avoided on account of the smell. He was going to die here just because someone figured it was cheaper to get convicts to cut timber than to pay for it to be done. He was going to die because he'd shot a man over a hand of cards. 'I didn't even kill him,' Harry would say, and then struggle for another breath.

'I'm going to the outhouse,' Leon said.

'Bring a jug of water back,' Bennett said. 'I'm as dry as a dead rattler.'

Bennett had a broken ankle. A log had fallen on his leg several months back. No one had set the leg properly and even though the bones were mending they had mended in such a way that it hurt him too much to walk. Twice or three times a day he made it to the outhouse, or to get water, but that was it. There was talk that they – the captain, the prison system, *someone* – wanted to send Bennett back to Huntsville but there was some issue with his broken leg. If he went back with the leg not treated properly the camp owners might get fined, or inspectors might turn up, or both. Bennett had been told they'd probably have to break the ankle again and then send him back with it freshly snapped. But the way this camp was, no one knew whether they were just telling him that to cause him mental anguish or if one day they were going to come for him with a hammer for his ankle and a stick for him to bite on.

'I'll come back for the jug,' Leon lied. 'I ain't carrying it into the hole.'

Leon stepped outside. The heat of the day was physical. It was a different heat to that inside the hut. Inside all of the air was warm but there was no one-place it came from. Outside, with the sun directly overhead, it was like standing in front of a raging fire. He took a breath of clean air, as he always did when first leaving the hut. He hitched his trousers up around his waist and started shuffling towards the outhouse.

In the distance he thought he heard someone shouting.

He could feel aches in his bones, tendons, and muscles, but most of all excitement, fear and hope coursing through his veins.

He looked up at the sky and his lips hardly moving he mouthed a prayer: *please God, let today be good.* After all that he had been through, please let this be his moment of redemption. *Amen.*

At the outhouse door he turned and looked back across the camp.

The lumber piles were burning.

White smoke was billowing upwards. There were tendrils of grey and great swathes of black amongst the white. Flames leapt skywards and he thought he could hear the crackle of burning. The guard called Billy was racing down towards the fire.

All that timber, all that work. The reason for them being here.

Leon smiled and opened the outhouse door.

He stepped behind the door, hiding himself from view if anyone was over by the gate watching him – but why would they be? Not with that great fire happening.

'You diamond, Jim Jackson,' he said aloud, and instead of entering the outhouse he stepped along the side, and looked down into the creek.

'Not so good,' he said. 'But what the hell.'

The creek was stagnant and stinking. Men's faeces were layered down there below the outhouse. A rat saw him and darted for cover upstream.

He'd been through worse. He slid down the side of the creek, managing to stop the slide before he landed in the dark water.

He crouched down as far as he could without dropping to his knees and, holding his breath, carefully manoeuvred his way through the piles of waste. The stink was worse than he'd imagined. The need to vomit was almost irresistible. Flies rose around him in a dark cloud. There was another rat. This one braver and not moving, just watching him, its tail and nose twitching, its teeth yellow. Leon clamped his own teeth together, balled his hands into fists, and forced himself to pass beneath the outhouse which most of the men had used only that morning.

At least it was cool under there, he thought, and had to stop himself opening his mouth as he laughed.

Four poles held the construction in place above him. One of them was rotting, he noticed. One of these days someone was going to be sat on the hole when the pole gave way and dumped the whole thing in the creek.

He wanted to laugh again, and now he recognized that it was nervousness and fear, not humour, that was causing the laughter. He trembled and, despite the smell, breathed rapidly through his clenched teeth.

Then, almost abruptly, the smell vanished and the air was clean and dry. The worst of the mess was behind him. The water was clean, and the steep banks of the creek were fresh and green.

Now he dropped to his knees, keeping his head and body as low as possible.

He began to crawl.

Webster Ellington looked across at the young railroad man and said, 'You knew, didn't you?'

Whittaker Gordon said, 'I knew he was coming after Leon Winters. I didn't know how. You?'

'About the same,' Ellington said. He looked to the south where the plume of smoke from the burning lumber piles hung high and impressively in the sky. Even against the wind one could hear the crackling of the fire and smell the burning.

'It's a good distraction,' Whit said.

'Yep.'

'Would probably have worked if we hadn't known.'

'Maybe,' Ellington said. But there wasn't really a maybe about it. The truth was, had he been none the wiser about Jim Jackson's plan to free Leon Winters he probably would have been caught up in trying to put the fire out. As it was, he'd sent Billy Burke down there. There wasn't anything that Billy could do, but at least it showed willing. It looked *right* if Jackson was watching.

'You think he's circled back round?' Whit said.

'Yep. See that creek – see where Winters is right now?'

They both looked over to the line of the stream. Winters was low in the gully and would have been easily missed if one hadn't been looking for him.

'Yep.'

'Follow it up to the fence. He'll fit under it, though he might get his knees wet. Then up the hill right to the tree line. That's where Jackson will be.'

'We going to go up there now?'

'No rush. Winters is struggling already. We've plenty of time.'

'Time for a cigarette?'

'Plenty,' Ellington said. 'Let's enjoy the show.'

They were gaining on him.

His horse had put her foot in a hole less than two miles away from the lumber yard and, although she was still making a good pace, she wasn't happy. When he looked back over his shoulder he was delighted to see the vast plume of white smoke rising up into the blue sky, and he was pleased – in a nervous way – to see the small shapes of two riders coming hell for leather after him. But he needed to get further away.

He pressed his heels into the horse's flanks and spoke reassuringly to her. She accelerated, but within minutes she was slowing again.

So he turned off the open trail and rode into the scrubland, where the rocks were higher, and where trees gave him cover. But there weren't enough trees for him to get lost in. The best he could hope for was to find a place where he could make a stand. There were only two chasers. Discover the right place and he ought to be able to draw them in, get them close enough, and . . . He thought again of the man breaking Rosalie's fingers.

Draw them in.

Get them close enough.

Yes, that was what he wanted.

It didn't really matter how much further he led them away from the camp. They wouldn't be going back anyway.

When Jim Jackson had set fire to the log piles and had set off southwards, Adams had said Jackson was no doubt going to circle back round to the high ground. 'We'll just keep following him,' Adams said.

But then Jackson had accelerated and had kept going south, further away from the camp.

George Dubois said, 'It doesn't look like he's circling around to me.'

Adams said. 'He's realized he's being followed.'

'What do we do?'

'We keep going. We've got him. This fire. The time he's been spent up here. It's enough.'

'Enough for what?'

'Enough to warrant whatever we do to him.'

She was limping now. With every step she took he could sense pain spiking up through her leg and into her shoulder. She was brave and loyal and still she pressed on, galloping as hard as she could. But he knew it was only a matter of time.

They rode into a wide ravine where rocks rose up steeply on either side. It wasn't ideal but it was the best he'd seen so far. He rode deeper into the ravine, slowing to a walk and then stopped altogether where two or three large boulders might offer him cover. Behind the boulders he could climb upwards and out of the ravine altogether if needs be.

He looked back to the entrance of the ravine. There was no sign yet of the two men following him but he knew they must be close.

He urged his horse forwards about twenty yards and left her standing free outside a second likely-looking hiding place, a natural cave, albeit too low to be perfect. It might confuse them and give him an edge.

Then he ran back to the three rocks that gave him better cover, pulling the Colt free of his holster as he went.

It was only when he was hidden behind one of the boulders, peering down the ravine, his face obscured by thick grass that had somehow found a way to grow in the cracks in the rock, that he wondered if he was capable of doing what he was planning.

The way it would work: the two men would ride into the gully and he would shoot them. But he'd never shot anyone in his life, not like that. Not from a hiding place. It would be akin to shooting a man in the back. It would be murder.

He couldn't see the smoke plume from where he stood, but he knew it was still there, hanging in the air, still expanding as the piles of logs burned. And what of Rosalie? Had she made it? Was she up there in the tree line waiting for Leon? And Leon? For all Jim Jackson knew Leon had been sent out on the work-party this very morning. Even if he had attempted to escape, could a man as weak and sick as Leon looked even crawl twenty yards let alone the few hundred he'd need to clear the fence and get all the way up to the tree line?

No, it was all crazy, too fanciful, too impossible. Jim realized now that what he should have done was to have ridden in there the first or second day when there was just one guard, maybe two, and shot them. Then he could have simply hauled Leon up on the back of the horse and be gone.

But he hadn't done that because it would have involved shooting innocent men.

Yet now he was going to have to do that anyway.

'*Except they ain't innocent,*' he said aloud through gritted teeth, his jawbone hardly moving. He thought of what they had done to Rosalie. One of them anyway. Although, who was to say it was that man that was coming after him?

It was all too confusing. He breathed out and realized that

he was thirsty. His hands were wet, and there was sweat on his forehead and neck, and his shirt was damp across his back. His whole body burned and the rock he was pressed up against had the morning's heat in it. The rock smelled dry and dusty, and now Jim's throat hurt and he had no spit when he swallowed. He peered around the other side of the rock and there was his grey, still standing in the middle of the trail, head down now as she ate some grass that she'd found, and he could see his waterskin on the back of the saddle.

It was too late.

He heard voices and when he looked back in the other direction they were here, pulling their horses up to a halt as they saw his grey.

The one in front raised his hand. He had a black beard. The man behind him drew a rifle from a scabbard on his saddle.

They sat there, horses unmoving, and scanned the trail ahead of them. Jim Jackson could see they were talking to one another but their voices never carried to him. They were too far away for a pistol shot even if he was prepared to kill a man from a hidden position.

Now the two men climbed off their horses and stood between the horses.

They walked forwards about ten yards, keeping all that horseflesh between themselves and the sides of the ravine.

They stopped.

Jim Jackson could only see their heads. The one with the beard was shaking his head. Now the other man handed Beardy his rifle.

Beardy raised the rifle.

Jim pressed himself hard up against the boulder. They can't have seen me, he thought. He was surely too well hidden.

He heard the rifle shot and he heard his horse cry out in pain. He looked and his horse was on her side, her head held upwards as she strained and struggled to understand what had just knocked her to the ground. She tried to stand, but her legs were confused. She managed to get halfway up, but then collapsed again, her chest heaving. He could hear her breathing and see the fear in her eyes as she looked back towards him. His left hand was balled into a tight fist and his right was trembling where he held the Colt. He breathed as rapidly as his horse, his body full of anger and sorrow and fear. The horse lay her head on the ground as the effort of fighting the pain became too much. He forced himself to control his own breathing, tried to focus on the moment, but he found himself thinking back to a few minutes earlier when she had been valiantly battling against her own pain to keep carrying him at the speed he wanted her. She'd always been like that. She had a personality of her own, could be obstinate sometimes and would often ignore him when other horses were around – like back in the stables in Austin, or even in the livestock carriage on that train that had brought him to Texas all those days ago – but she had always done her best for him with a dedication that he'd never found in any other horse. These last few days she had covered so many miles and had never once complained. She was looking in his direction and it was a few moments before he realized she was no longer breathing, her eyes wide and white, but very still.

He turned back to the two men.

There was now just one man hiding between the horses – Beardy. The second man was scrabbling up the rocks on the opposite side of the gully. He had the rifle back from Beardy now, and was keeping low, working from one boulder to another, looking nervously around, but getting higher and higher all the time.

Meanwhile, a step at a time, Beardy worked his way deeper into the small canyon.

Leon Winters crawled beneath the camp fence.

The wire fence was laid straight across the top of the creek from one bank to another, when whoever had constructed it should really have brought the fence down the banks and cross the creek at water level. The way it was, anyone could crawl beneath it.

But, Leon figured, why would anyone even try it?

That's why whoever had put the fence up hadn't been very diligent. Under normal circumstances anyone crawling this far would have been spotted way back. Certainly anyone strong enough to make it this far would normally have been out on the cutting gang and when they were back in camp the guards would have been more numerous and more observant.

But with the fire raging across camp and only the sick men still inside, the circumstances were perfect.

Except that his strength was failing him. His hands were bleeding where he had pressed down on numerous flints and stones, and the water, what little there was, had soaked through his trousers. Every time he placed his bony knees on the ground he grimaced. His shoulders ached, the midday heat was making him sweat and he had no drinking water. Now he could feel the world starting to spin and he had to lower his head and pause for breath. He conjured up all the terrors of the last dozen years, all the injustices, all the humiliations and the agonies. He thought of Jim Jackson out there, setting all of this up just for him, for Leon. And somehow all of this gave him enough strength to make it another yard. Then one more. But up ahead the slope steepened. The tree line was impossibly far away. And thus the pattern started again, finding inner strength, making one more yard.

Again and again and again.

'I bet he stinks,' Webster Ellington said. 'The way he dropped down beneath the outhouse and now he's crawled all that way in the hot sun.'

Whit Gordon said, 'We going to ride up there now?'

'Yes. I guess it's time. We take it easy though. Slow and

quiet. Jim Jackson's the one we want. Jackson is up there waiting for him. Soon as the two of them are together we grab them.'

The bullet smashed into the rock behind Jim Jackson's head, showering him with stone splinters. He pressed himself hard up against the boulder that shielded him and he heard the man high on the rocks opposite shout 'There he is! Watch for my shot.'

A second bullet ploughed into the stone behind him.

'I see him,' Beardy said.

Jim Jackson raised his Colt and held it at face level. He took a deep breath, released the air slowly, and then quickly, without aiming, leaned out low and fired a shot towards Beardy.

The man ducked behind his horse.

'You should come out,' Beardy called. 'At least that way you get to stay alive.'

'You shot my horse,' Jim shouted back.

'Where you're going, you won't need a horse.'

'You shot my horse,' Jim said, quieter this time, as if it was all the reason he needed for anything that might follow.

Across the trail he heard a scrabbling movement. He risked a quick glance. The man over there was up on the top of the wall of rocks and he was working his way further along the ravine. Soon Jim wouldn't be able to peer around that side of his boulder for risk of being shot.

It wasn't meant to be this way. He'd had visions of out-running them, leading them far enough away that he could lose them and then circle back. Or had he been secretly hoping for a confrontation? Either way, he hadn't thought it through. He was trapped and, although he'd back himself to kill two men in a straight shootout, he knew it wasn't going to turn out that way. They were going to outflank him and kill him where he stood or force him out into the open and surrender.

'Throw your gun out, Jackson,' Beardy called.

They know who I am, he thought. It killed any lingering doubt that Beardy was the same man who had broken Rosalie's fingers. He felt something inside glowing with anger and purpose, a determination that whatever happened here he would somehow exact revenge for both Rosalie and his horse.

'You broke a woman's fingers,' he said.

The other thing he had to do was to keep them here for as long as he could. The more time they were here the better chances Rosalie and Leon had. But that fellow opposite was still working his way down the canyon. It would only be minutes before Jim's position was compromised.

'How do you know that?' Beardy said, and Jim Jackson cursed himself. Had he just revealed that Rosalie was in town? But at least the man hadn't denied it. And he was closer now. His voice was quieter.

Jim risked another quick look.

If the man was twenty yards nearer – and he was still moving, crouching down behind the horse, urging her forwards – then Jim may very well have a shot. He could step out, aim, and fire. It would be one shot. The fellow upon the rocks opposite would get him for sure.

One shot. Revenge.

Just a few more seconds.

But he'd misjudged.

He heard the gunshot at exactly the same time as he felt the punch in his lower right calf. His leg buckled beneath him and he fell against the rock, almost dropping his Colt. He looked down and saw the tear in his trousers, the blood on the stone behind him.

'I got him!' the man yelled. 'Legged him.'

Jim Jackson used his left leg to lever himself fully behind the boulder just as the man opposite fired again. This bullet splintered the rock where his wounded leg had been a second earlier.

Then came the pain.

Just a small wave to start with, as if the ocean tide had just turned and the water was rolling gently over the sand. But then arrived a larger, stronger wave, then another, and suddenly it was as if his leg had been immersed in a boiling raging sea.

He pressed himself hard up against the boulder, riding the waves of pain, gritting his teeth, trying to slow his breathing. He was aware that the man opposite was still moving, still looking for a line of sight, and that the man down there, Beardy, who had shot his horse and tortured his woman . . . *his* woman . . . was edging closer too. He could feel blood filling his boot. His vision wavered. His throat was too dry. He squeezed his eyes closed and reopened them. He ought to tie something around his leg or press something against the wound to stop the flow, otherwise he would bleed to death, but he had no room to manoeuvre.

'Throw your gun out,' Beardy said, his voice quiet but strong. 'You got two minutes. George over there's got you clean in his sights now.'

He'd never considered Rosalie his woman before. The thought had come to him in these desperate moments, these last moments. They had shot his horse and tortured his woman.

'Minute and a half,' Beardy said. 'You'll go to prison but at least you'll be alive.'

Jim Jackson's chest heaved. He thought of Leon somewhere back up the camp. He thought of Rosalie. Would the two of them make it back to the farm he had told her about, a deserted place he had found a few days earlier? Would they be able to outrun a posse or hide for long enough? And then what about the thing that this had all been for? Neither of them knew about the fellow McRae had told him about back in New Mexico. It felt like a lifetime ago. What had been the fellow's name? Jack Anderson in Leyton, Texas. Jim's vision wavered again and in the wavering he pictured Rosalie across the table from him in Austin saying 'John Allan. Allan with an A. No records of him.' He thought of John Allan now. A thin scarred man. Rarely smiled. It suddenly seemed so important that Rosalie and Leon knew about Leyton, Texas. That was what this had all been about. Well, not only that. It had been about freeing Leon from the same hell that Jim himself had been through, but on the back of that it was about understanding who had framed them and put them there.

'One minute,' Beardy said, his voice quiet but hard. 'Prison or death. The choice is yours.'

CHAPTER SEVENTEEN

Leon Winters looked at the pretty woman standing next to two horses and said, 'Who are you?'

His bones ached. His muscles were beyond pain. He was soaked with sweat and creek water and from blood where the sharp stones and flints had cut his hands and his legs and his arms on those occasions when he had slipped or when his hands had simply given way. He was struggling for breath and his vision was blurred – he didn't know if it was tears, blood, exhaustion or any combination of these.

He knelt on the ground, feeling the softness of grass and dead leaves, smelling the freshness of trees and he looked up at the two horses and at the woman.

She was beautiful, slim and young, smiling at him with pretty eyes and red lips, and he thought that he'd never seen a woman look so good. Truth was, there had been many times over the last few years when he thought he'd never see a woman again, let alone one so angelic.

'I'm not dead, am I?' he said, only half in jest.

'I'm Rosalie.'

It was just like Jim to send a woman for him.

'Where's Jim?'

'He's busy elsewhere.'

'The fire.'

'Yes.'

The way the high sun was catching her face she looked pale. There was a worried line to her mouth, too.

'Can you stand?'

Even as she was asking the question she was crouching down, holding his hand, hers soft and warm, and helping him up. He grimaced in pain.

'Are you OK?'

'Better than I have been for years.'

'Can you climb on the horse?'

Again, it wasn't really a question, more an invitation, and already she was helping him, supporting him – hell, almost leveraging him – up on to the saddle. He moaned aloud. His legs hurt like they'd been whipped – which had happened many times – and his belly, spine, and shoulders all sent shards of pain from one body part to another. It was as if there was a whirlwind of agony inside him.

'Are you OK?' she asked again.

'My ears and toes don't hurt,' he said. 'On second thoughts, my toes do.'

She smiled as she climbed on to her own horse and the smile helped with the pain.

'Where are we going?' he asked.

'There's a place. It's a few miles away, apparently.'

'Apparently? You've not been there?'

'I have directions. Jim said it's derelict and hidden – over-grown. He's got food and water there.'

'First place the posse will look.'

'No, Jim said it's well off any trail and it's hidden.'

'Let's hope we can find it, then' he said, and smiled. Being on a horse again felt good whatever happened. Especially with Rosalie. 'Lead the way,' he said.

'Let 'em ride,' Webster Ellington whispered. 'We can take

them anytime.'

'You mean wait for Jim Jackson to join them?'

'Yep, that's what I mean.'

They let the girl and Winters ride on ahead. When they figured the couple was far enough away that they wouldn't be spotted, they followed. It was a good day, Webster Ellington figured. The sun felt nice on his shoulders and it was good to be out riding through the trees with a nice cooling breeze on one's face. It was a good day that was going to get better.

Beardy said, 'Thirty seconds.'

Jim was on the verge of throwing his gun out and stepping from cover. The man opposite had moved far enough along the ridge that Jim could see him – which meant the man could see Jim. Blood was still running from Jim's leg, and the pain was filling all of his body. He was breathing too fast, panting almost. The memories of his own experiences in the Texas prison camps started appearing in his mind: the beatings, the dreaded leather strapped bat, the hunger and the cold. He'd always known that he would do anything to avoid going back to such a place. It would kill him. He knew that with a certainty that sent a chill through the fire that was filling his body. Yet there was still some sense of self-preservation that made him consider throwing his gun out and limping, maybe crawling, out there.

At least he'd be alive for a little while longer.

He thought of Rosalie and of Leon. It had been too ambitious. It had been crazy.

'Ten seconds!' Beardy shouted.

Jim Jackson sighed and lowered the Colt. It was all over. Life was all over. Rosalie. Leon. Even Jennifer back east. It was over.

A gunshot exploded from across the ravine. Jim heard the man over there cry out. Jim snatched a quick look. The man was standing up, no longer interested in Jim, but instead looking mystified, and searching blindly for balance on the slope.

'That one's for Ned,' someone yelled – a new voice. Then there was another shot and Jim Jackson saw blood explode from the back of the man's head and he tumbled face-forward down the rocks. At the bottom of the slope he lay still.

Jim pressed himself tight up against the rock again.

'And this one's because you broke my fingers,' a second new voice said. There were two more shots in quick succession. He heard someone swear: Beardy.

You broke my fingers.

Jim racked his brains trying to figure out who these new people might be. But there was nothing. Besides, it wasn't time to think. It was time to act. He turned and started to scrabble up the narrow cleft in the rock face behind him. It wasn't steep and should have been as easy as climbing a staircase, but his right leg wasn't obeying orders and he couldn't put any weight on it.

He glanced backwards.

He was in the open now and they could see him as clearly as he could see them. But they weren't looking. Beardy was on his back. There was blood on the ground around him and he was breathing heavily. The horses either side of him that he had been sheltering between had moved away, presumably frightened by the gunshots. Beardy's gun lay on the dirt a few feet from his outstretched arm. Jim saw now that Beardy had been shot in the shoulder. Walking towards Beardy was a man Jim hadn't seen before; a thin man with red stubble on his face. The man had a gun in his hand.

'Boss, Jackson's getting away.'

The second man had a rifle in his hand. He was standing at the bottom of the far rock wall, over by one of the horses, and he was looking right at Jim.

He knows my name, too, Jim thought.

The man with the red stubble looked away from Beardy and glanced up at Jim.

Jim saw it happening.

141

Beardy reached inside his jacket with his left hand, his good hand. Maybe he had a shoulder holster in there, Jim thought.

Red said 'It's OK; he's bleeding. He ain't going nowhere. We'll catch him in a moment and, anyway, I want to spend some time with him on account of Little Joe.'

He looked back down at Beardy and his eyes widened in realization of his mistake. Beardy now had a gun in his hand. Without hesitation Beardy shot Red in the face.

Red was blown backwards, his hat flying off to reveal a head of red hair, and he lay still.

Beardy moved fast. He rolled over – on to his wounded shoulder – aimed and fired at the other man in one slick movement.

The other man was equally fast. He'd moved the rifle's aim from Jim to Beardy and fired in the same movement.

The gunshots were simultaneous.

Both men cried out in pain.

The man with the rifle staggered backwards, his mouth open in an 'O' shape. There was a bloom of blood on his chest. He tried to raise the rifle for a second shot, but his hands appeared to lose all of their power and the rifle slipped to the ground. He fell and was motionless.

The rifle bullet had taken Beardy in the stomach. He lay on his wounded arm facing the man he had just shot. Jim could see that his lower back was a mass of blood and torn clothes where the rifle bullet had exited the body. As he watched, the man rolled slowly on to his back. He lay in a growing pool of his own blood, his chest heaving and eyes looking up at the endless blue sky.

Jim's own pain was forgotten for a moment. His heart raced and his hands shook. It felt as if he had been involved in that brief gunfight himself. But no, it wasn't that. He had been ten seconds away from giving it all up. Cornered and helpless, ten seconds of real living had been all that had remained and then . . . what had just happened? Four men dead or dying and he was still standing.

He took in the whole scene. Beardy was still breathing but the other men weren't moving. It may have been imagination but it seemed that he could still hear the echoes of the gun-shots bouncing back and forth between the rock walls of the ravine.

He carefully climbed back down to the boulder he had been hiding behind. He stepped out on to the trail, all the time watching Beardy. He'd seen him surprise the hell out of the red-haired man and wasn't about to make the same mistake.

Beardy was moaning in agony and now Jim's own pain returned. He sat on the ground and looked at his wound. The bullet had entered his leg just above the top of his boot. He didn't think it had hit the bone, but there was a lot of blood and the flesh was torn.

He pulled his neckerchief from around his neck and folded it into a long rectangle and he pressed it against the wound. It felt like a series of hot knives had been plunged into his leg from ankle to groin. The world wavered in front of him. He took off his jacket and his shirt and he ripped the sleeves off the latter and then he tied the folded neckerchief tight against the wound with the torn sleeves. He put his ruined shirt and his jacket back on and tried to stand.

More agony. But he could put up with it.

He held his gun out in front of him, his finger tight on the trigger, and he limped towards Beardy, the man who had shot his horse and tortured his woman.

The cabin had been reclaimed by the forest. Whoever had farmed the area had constructed the cabin out of pine logs that had been cut from the forest behind. The land in front of the house had been cleared of stones and carved into small fields. The stones had been mixed with wet clay and had been used to build the low walls of a stable that had then been topped with more pine logs. The farmhouse roof had also been made from logs, criss-crossed with thick interlaced pine branches and on top of that a layer of soil.

But now the fields were barely recognizable: grass had grown back long and thick, bushes and weeds had sprouted and multiplied and, closer to the woods, young trees were growing as if breaking out from the shelter of their parents. Many of these young trees obscured the farm cabin. Closer to the forest were several older trees that looked like they had marched out of the woods and had stationed themselves around the cabin. Grass had grown in the soil on the roof and log tendrils of weeds and wild flowers hung down. The stable walls had collapsed and the roof, no longer straight, appeared to grow out of the ground.

From the westbound trail, skirting the edge of another wood half a mile away, the cabin was invisible.

'Don't cut across the fields towards the cabin,' Jim had told her. 'You won't see it anyway, so you'd have no reason to cut across. You'll come to a creek. There's a doll – an Indian doll, you know, coloured beads and bright face? It's impaled on a tree with an arrow.'

'A doll?'

'I didn't put it there. I don't know why it's there. Maybe it's an Indian sign that there's a farm nearby. Or maybe the farmer did it to warn them off. Anyway, it was what made me stop and look around. I figured there must be something close. Follow the creek through the woods to the left – just ride in the water. It runs behind the old farm. Might be wise to take the doll down. Without it there's no reason to pause. Anyone else will ride straight by.'

Rosalie had struggled to remove the doll – the arrow was too deeply embedded into the tree. In the end she had torn the doll off the shaft. Without the doll drawing attention to the tree it would take an eagle-eyed posse member to spot the arrow. And even if they did, so what? And that was always

144

assuming they'd come this way anyway. There had been so many trails and forks, so many possibilities, that the chances of them being found seemed incredibly remote.

She and Leon rode through the creek and at the farm-house they found water and food left there by Jim.

She felt an enormous pang of fear. He'd planned it all so well, set everything up so carefully. But what if he had been caught? What if all of this was for nothing? What if she never saw him again?

Leon must have sensed her mood or seen the worry on her face because he said, 'Some people have luck riding on their shoulders, Rosalie. Jim's one of them. I've always thought it was because he's a good man. God looks after the good ones.'

She looked at him and managed to smile.

They hid the horses in the stables – there was even a sack of oats left there – and then she and Leon ate jerky, onions and thick crusts of bread in the farmhouse.

'Best meal I've had in a dozen years,' Leon said, slicing another wedge of bread with a long knife that, despite looking like it had been in the cabin since the day the place had been built, was still strong and sharp.

Rosalie ate well, too. She hadn't thought she'd be hungry, but it turned out she was ravenous.

Later, she stood looking out of the window – real glass, no less. Trees and hanging branches obscured her view. She turned back to Leon. 'Tell me about Jim,' she said. 'Tell me about yourself. Tell me everything.'

Jim Jackson pushed Beardy's gun away from the dying man with the toe of his good leg. He figured the man wouldn't have a second hidden weapon but it was a chance not worth taking, so all the while he pointed his own gun right at the man's face. There was blood frothing from Beardy's mouth now.

'Who were they?' Beardy asked, looking up at him.

'No idea. Figured you knew.'

'We'd have had you if they hadn't come along.'

Beardy coughed up a fountain of blood.

'You had to break a woman's fingers to get this far.'

Beardy tried to say something but he coughed up more blood. He grimaced in pain. Then said, 'You've the luck of the Devil riding with you.'

'You shot my horse,' Jim said. 'I'm going to take yours.'

'Shoot me,' Beardy said. 'Please.'

'I've never shot a man I didn't have to,' Jim said, and walked away.

Leon told her a little of the train-robbing days, and of how Jim came to be known as the gentleman train robber. He recounted how Jim had told him he was giving it all up and that the next time he heard from Jim was when the little boy handed him the secret note in the outhouse. Rosalie asked him about life in the camp but Leon just shook his head. 'It's not something to talk about,' he said.

She heard one of the horses in the hidden stable neigh.

'How long do you think he'll be?' she said

A man appeared in the doorway. He had a shotgun in his hand that he was aiming right at Rosalie.

He said, 'I was just wondering the very same thing.'

CHAPTER EIGHTEEN

His name, he told them, was Webster Ellington.

'*Captain* Webster T. Ellington,' he said. 'I was a captain and I'm pretty darn sure that I will be again once we bring all three of you in.'

A younger man, lean, medium height, and quiet, was with Ellington. He'd brought a coil of thin rope into the room with him and wore a six-gun. Ellington had the man check Rosalie and Leon for weapons and then he made the two of them sit on the bench facing him, their backs to the table.

'Whit,' he said to the younger man. 'I want you to go outside. Move our horses so they're way out of sight. Then hide up yourself. When Jackson arrives you be behind him. Follow him in and be ready. Be silent.'

'Sure.'

'Hit him upside the head. He'll be looking at me. Hit him just above the ear as hard as you can. When he wakes up. . . .'

Ellington grinned as he gave the orders. The situation appeared to be making him very happy. It was making Rosalie feel sick. Fear and terrible desperate disappointment added to her nausea.

She was searching for something – anything – that she could use as a weapon, but there was nothing. Leon was looking pale, tired, and ghostlike alongside her. She could feel him shivering.

'Yes, you shake, boy,' Ellington said. 'You shake like a whipped dog because you know what's coming, don't you?'

'It's not over yet,' Leon whispered.

'That's why I'm savouring the moment,' Ellington said. 'This is . . . wonderful. Don't you think?'

Outside they heard a horse neigh again. 'He's from the railroad,' Ellington explained. 'The one you robbed.'

'I've not robbed anyone for twelve years. You know that.'

'I never said when.' Ellington licked his lips and smiled again.

He looked at Rosalie. 'I don't know what you have to do with all of this but I'm afraid it ain't going to hurt me or Whit one bit to have caught you, too, ma'am. See, this is going to put me right back where I belong.'

He turned to Leon. 'Sad thing for you is, once they've finished with you, I'm going to insist that sooner or later you and Jackson both come back to me – wherever I am by then. We have some unfinished business, don't we? Well, especially Jackson. But I'd hate for you to miss out. You do look a bit . . . weak though. I wonder how much you can take?'

'You're evil,' Leon said.

'What unfinished business?' Rosalie asked. She wasn't sure she wanted to know, but the man was loud and getting louder. She thought if she kept him talking Jim might – just *might* – hear him as he approached. It wasn't much. But it was all she had.

'Well, it's interesting you ask. See, they wanted him dead. But I never killed him. And for that. . . . Well, I got demoted and sent to one dead-end rat-infested camp after another. It wasn't my fault he didn't die. I mean, I wasn't going to *kill* him, was I? Despite what Leon here thinks, I'm not evil. I'm not bad. I'm just doing my job the way they ask. Jackson was meant to die, and he didn't and they blamed me. It spoiled my life. Wife left me on account of the places they sent me were no places for wives. Now's my chance to make amends.'

'Who wanted him dead?'

'I don't know, lady. They. The authorities. Him, too.' He pointed at Leon. 'He was meant to die, too. Look at him. He's close. But they seem to have charmed lives, these train robbers.'

'And what are you going to do with us?'

'Well, as soon as Jackson turns up I'll be taking you all back down the hill with me. After that I might just take me a ride into town to celebrate.'

'He won't be taken alive,' Leon said.

'He won't know he's still alive until he wakes up.'

'You don't know him as well as you think.'

'Oh I do. When you've seen a man scream and cry and soil himself as many times as I've seen Jackson, then you get to know him very well. He'll look at me and freeze. He always did.'

'He's changed.'

'Then it's a good job Whit is out there,' Ellington said. 'Now let me get comfortable. I guess he could be an hour or two, the way things were back at the camp.'

She had taken the doll off the tree just as he'd told her. That was good. It meant that she'd found the place. More than that, it meant they she and Leon were here, that the plan had worked. After a fashion, anyway. There were four men dead back in the ravine south of the camp. He didn't know who they all were and – though he figured they probably deserved to die and had brought it on themselves – it was almost certainly a higher body count than would have happened if he had just ridden into the camp, grabbed Leon, and shot his way out. But then that way the dead may well have been innocent. His horse was dead, too. He'd limped over to her and had stroked her cooling head.

There had been no time to change saddles, and his horse had been lying on her side and he hadn't the strength in his

149

weakening body to move her. He had grabbed his bag, his water, his remaining money and the telescope, and he had taken one of the dead men's horses, a fine looking black. The wound in his leg throbbed with every heartbeat, and with every step the horse took a fresh stab of pain shot up his body.

But the doll was gone and that meant Rosalie and Leon had made it this far. Now he had made it this far.

He allowed himself a smile.

Rosalie hated what she was hearing – all this talk of whippings and beatings and of breaking a man so deeply that he cried at the mere mention of the bat. It was so desperately hard to hear and she wondered if she would ever see Jim Jackson in the same way again, without pity, without shame for what her fellow human beings were capable of. But Ellington was loud. He revelled in the stories so much that his voice got louder and his laughter boomed out and all Rosalie could do was to pray that Jim Jackson heard. So whenever Ellington's tales faltered she prompted him for more.

Then suddenly he went quiet. He stopped mid-flow and put a finger across his lips. He rose from the chair he'd been relaxing in and stood up against the far wall of the cabin, facing the door, the shotgun pointing at Rosalie over to his right, who was still sitting on the hard bench in front of the table.

Outside the horses snorted. Rosalie felt faint. The cabin was dusty and the late afternoon air was warm and dry in her throat. She coughed and Ellington glared at her. The room smelled of body heat. At some point – and she had no idea when it had happened – hers and Leon's fingers had become entwined. She squeezed his hand now and she looked at him. He was tired and exhausted. There were beads of sweat on his forehead. Earlier the action, excitement, and energy that the bid for freedom had created had kept him going, but this last hour, he had become pale and quiet, shuddering despite the heat, eyes closed against some of Ellington's more vicious stories.

A shadow passed by the dirty window.

'You made it,' Jim Jackson said from just outside the door. 'We *all* made it.'

Jim Jackson opened the door to the cabin and stepped inside.

You couldn't out-draw a man who already had a gun in his hand.

It wasn't creed or code; it was simple truth, a truth borne out of logic and mechanics as much as anything. If the other fellow only had to squeeze the trigger and you had to reach for a gun, raise that gun, and pull the trigger, then he was going to kill you.

So Jim Jackson came through the door with his gun in his hand and his finger on the trigger. He had told himself he wouldn't hesitate. That all he had was a split second of grace and in that time he had to kill Ellington. He had to become what he had always feared he would become – a cold-hearted killer.

He couldn't do it.

He paused.

He hesitated.

And in that moment Ellington laughed, spit spraying from the man's mouth, a sneer on his mocking lips.

It was the gun pointing at Rosalie. If the gun had been pointing towards the door, towards him, then he'd have killed Ellington and taken his chances with the man's dying reflexes. But the shotgun, and all those thousands of shards of lead, each one a tiny white-hot knife, would have peppered her, ruined her, blinded her.

So he paused and Ellington laughed.

'Jim,' Rosalie said. 'I'm so sorry.'

'Jim Jackson,' Webster Ellington said. 'After all this time we meet again.'

Leon said, 'Jim.'

Jim stood in the doorway, his finger applying pressure to the Colt's trigger. His leg hurt. The world seemed slightly off-kilter as if there was a slight mist and a slight tilt to everything. He could hear his own breathing. It was harsh and fast and his lungs burned.

'Put the gun down, Jackson,' Ellington said.

'No.'

If Ellington moved his shotgun, started to swing it towards Jackson, then Jim would shoot. That's what he told himself. But would he? *Could* he?

Sunlight came in through the window. It was low and golden and the dust in the air and the way the sunlight landed on Rosalie's hair took him back to the moment in the railway carriage when he had first seen her.

She and Leon were sat on a bench against a table by the window. Ellington was standing at the end of the bench facing the door, still with the gun pointing towards Rosalie.

'You can't kill me without me killing the girl,' Ellington said.

'Maybe,' Jim said. 'Maybe not.'

Ellington smiled. 'We just going to stand here then?'

Leon could see it happening – could *imagine* it. This face off, the two of them staring at one another, and Jim having no idea that at any time the other one was sneaking up quietly ready to smash him on the side of the head and knock him out cold.

Leon couldn't bear it. The thought of going back to the camp. All those things that Ellington had just been saying, all the tortures and humiliations. He – Ellington – had been enjoying making Rosalie squirm with his disgusting and vile descriptions and promises. Ellington had seemingly loved the way her breath had become short and tears had sprung from her eyes. The way she had had to hide her mouth with her hand at the worst of the descriptions. But they were all true.

None of it was exaggeration. It was what had happened. It was what *would* happen again. He couldn't go back there. Not after today. Not after the hope and the fresh air and the moments of freedom, of seeing Rosalie for the first time like an angel in the trees, of those first minutes in this cabin, of cutting the bread and eating and believing it had all worked. That somehow, despite all the odds, Jim Jackson had made it work.

Cutting the bread.

Look at Jim now. He was swaying. One leg was dark with blood. He'd bandaged it roughly but the bandage was all soaked through. There was blood on his face, too, and all down his shirt and jacket front. Lots of blood. But it didn't hide how pale and how weary Jim looked. His eyes were dark, sunken into the shadows beneath his hat, but Leon could see the tiredness there. Jim was breathing fast, too, as if his body was building up to one final moment of effort.

Leon let go of Rosalie's hand. She tried to hold on to his fingers but he pulled his hand away, trying to make the movement surreptitious.

'The gun, Jackson,' Ellington said. 'Best you put it down before you drop it. You're looking might tired and if I ain't mistaken you're losing a lot of blood.'

He was playing for time, Leon knew. Any second now Whit would appear and with one blow – and it looked like it wouldn't have to be much of a blow – he would lay Jim out.

'I should just shoot you,' Jim said.

'Mmm,' Ellington said, and raised the shotgun towards Rosalie's face. 'You just try it.'

Something moved outside.

It may have been a branch scratching on the cabin roof, Leon thought later. But right then he pictured Whit sliding up behind Jim with his gun reversed in his hand, ready to knock Jim out.

Leon reached behind and on the table he felt a plate. He touched an onion and then an old clay cup he had been drinking water from. His fingers found bread.

His hand grasped the bread knife.

He took a deep breath.

He lunged for Webster T. Ellington.

Leon's move caught them all by surprise.

Ellington sensed the movement and he turned as Leon rose from the bench and thrust the knife forwards. Ellington leaned backwards, the movement becoming a step, and he started to lower the shotgun, the barrel aim moving from Rosalie to Leon.

'No!' Jim cried.

Then Leon was beneath the shotgun barrel, his shoulder knocking the gun upwards as Ellington pulled the trigger. Suddenly he was upon the prison guard, driving the knife deep into the man's gut, hearing the man scream and the roar of the shotgun blast deafening him. He smelt gunpowder and felt smoke in his eyes and warm blood on his hands. Then there were two more shots, shots felt rather than heard because his ears were already dulled, and he felt Ellington's body lifted momentarily away from him, the knife still embedded in the man's belly, and then Ellington was sliding down the cabin wall. He could hear a woman screaming far away, and he turned; Jim's gun was smoking. Leon said, 'Jim, there's another one. He's going to sneak up behind you' and then his vision wavered as if all that energy that he had used in the last few seconds was all that he'd had left inside, and he succumbed to the darkness, too.

CHAPTER NINETEEN

Jim Jackson said, 'I'd made a promise to the boy – Alfie. I said if he gave you the note then I'd give him the telescope.'

'He kept his half of the bargain,' Leon said.

'I was watching when he gave you the note. Once I set the log piles burning and . . . After the trouble down in the canyon it seemed like the most stupid thing in the world for me to ride back up close to the camp. I should have just headed up here. But I'd made a promise.'

Leon nodded as if he understood, either about the promise itself or about how Jim felt about the promise.

Rosalie was quiet. She had a blanket wrapped around her shoulders but couldn't stop shivering.

'So I rode back up through the trees and worked my way to the place where I'd met Alfie yesterday.'

'And he was there?'

'Yes, he was. He was there watching the fire and watching the guard running about but most of all he was waiting for me.'

Rosalie said, 'He knew you'd keep your word.'

'Yes. So I gave him the telescope and he was so excited and he said to me, "I gave Leon the note like you said." I told him that I knew he would. He said, "Leon escaped. Was that what was in the note?" I told him that it might have been but that he must never ever tell anyone, that it was a secret he had to keep forever. I asked him if he could do that and he said, "Sure. I'm good at secrets." Then he said, "Webster was waiting though. Him and that new man. They watched Leon crawl all the way up the creek and they was waiting for him at the top".'

'They were watching me?' Leon said.

'Alfie said, "Are you all right?" And I had to pretend that my heart hadn't just exploded in my chest. "They were waiting?" I asked, and Alfie said, "Yes. I was watching them watching Leon. They didn't grab 'em, though. Leon and a pretty woman. They followed. That's all I saw so I came down here and waited for you".'

'So you *knew*?' Rosalie said.

'I know *something*. I knew not to come rushing in.'

Leon looked over at Jim. 'And the other fellow? Whit?'

Rosalie said, 'He was going to sneak in behind you and knock you out.'

'What happened to him?' Leon said.

Jim Jackson shook his head.

CHAPTER TWENTY

They hid out for two weeks.

Jim Jackson had stockpiled food for them and the horses. They supplemented this with wild onions and potatoes that were still growing in the old fields, and with rabbit and squirrel that Leon trapped with wire snares they found in the stables. The creek water was clean, cold and refreshing.

Leon grew stronger every day. Jim's leg wound healed. They re-bandaged and re-splinted Rosalie's fingers.

Each night Leon took a watch outside in the woods and after several hours Jim took over. Only once, during the day, did they see riders approaching. But the riders were several fields away and passed by without realizing that there was a cabin hidden in the woods.

At the times when Leon was on watch Jim Jackson and Rosalie talked, but there was awkwardness to their conversation that hadn't been there before. They could both sense that everything else was still there, but the awkwardness sat on top of it all, preventing either of them getting to anything else.

'You're an outlaw now,' Jim said one night. 'I mean, really. Look at us – holed up in a hideaway waiting for bullet wounds to heal. We're wanted right across the state. If they ever catch me now, I'll hang. Leon, too. I'm sorry. I never meant for it to be like this.'

He could see the sheen of tears in her eyes reflecting the

faint moonlight that made it through the dirty window.

'I wouldn't have changed a thing,' she said.

They were lying together, underneath a blanket on the hard floor.

'It's just. . . .'

'It's just what?' he said.

'Something *has* changed.'

'If it's me—'

'No, it's not you. Well, maybe you've changed a little. But it's not that.'

'What is it?'

'It's knowledge.'

'Knowledge?'

'Before you came in . . . Before . . . That man had spent an hour telling us – telling *me*, because Leon already knew – what he had done to you. I mean, *exactly* what he had done to you. And what he was going to do. It was . . . awful. Jim . . . I'm so sorry.'

'It's not your fault.'

'How can people be like that? I just never realized what you had been through.'

'It's OK.'

'It's not. And now we're separated by this awfulness, this experience that you've had and that I will never – thankfully – know.'

'Please, forget it. It's done. I'm never going back.'

'I would have killed him straight away. You paused. Despite everything you still paused because it wouldn't have given him a fair chance. Jim, I just think. . . . You're too good.' She had laughed and cried, and they had kissed, and that had been the start of it being good again.

They buried Webster T. Ellington, and one night Jim buried the young man whose name was Whit. He had wrapped Whit's body in canvas that he had found at the back of the cabin. As he was shovelling soil into the grave Jim sensed someone watching.

'Leon,' he said, pausing, resting.

'I still haven't thanked you.'

'Yes you have. A hundred times. Every day.'

'You never said what happened.' Leon nodded at the grave.

Jim shook his head again.

Leon said, 'I know that it's eating you up, Jim. I can see it in your eyes. Hear it in your voice.'

'It's OK.'

'Sometimes self-defence doesn't always look like self-defence.'

'What does that mean?'

'It means that if I had known what you had known – that Rosalie and I had been followed up here – and if I had been carefully sneaking towards the cabin because I didn't know what I was going to find and I had come across someone watching out for me; if I had had to crawl up behind that man and maybe cut his throat because I needed to be quiet and there was no other way for it to be done; if I had had to do that, I wouldn't be torturing myself over it being murder in cold blood or anything. I'd sleep well because it was self-defence.'

Jim looked at Leon. The moonlight illuminated his face. Leon was looking stronger now.

'Thanks Leon.'

'I saw all the blood,' Leon said, 'on your shirt and jacket. I didn't realize at first what it meant.'

'It doesn't sit easy. Maybe it never will. It feels like something has changed. Like I've crossed a line that's wider than the Missouri.'

'Like I said, sometime self-defence isn't as obvious as we would like it to be.'

Jim Jackson looked up at the night sky, at the stars, at whatever infinity lay behind. Then he turned back to earth and shovelled a load of dirt on to the grave of the young man whose throat he had cut.

'Tomorrow we should move out, Leon. We've a man to hunt.'

'And Rosalie?'

'She's with us. We're outlaws now. All of us. For good or bad.'